Praise for *Strangers I Know*

"Blending fiction, essay, and memoir, this narrative . . . encompasses autobiographical e   , and current events. At its hea   matic parents, both deaf, who   o return. . . . Her inventive a   f the characters, while respecti

—*The New Yorker*

"*Strangers I Know* lies at the intersection of memoir, literary criticism, and bildungsroman, bleeding fiction into fact in order to explore the mythologies that have shaped Durastanti's life and sensibility. . . . Symphonic."

—*The Paris Review*

"Part documentary, part fiction, part literary criticism . . . a coming-of-age story spiked with the same brand of vitriol that springs up from works like Greta Gerwig's *Lady Bird* and Virginia Woolf's *A Room of One's Own*."

—*The Observer* (London)

"Wonderfully translated by Elizabeth Harris . . . For Durastanti, language has the power to perform an excavation of the self in the attempt to bring the inexpressible into understanding."

—*Ploughshares*

"Incisive and profound, *Strangers I Know* is a tremendous work by Durastanti and translator Elizabeth Harris. . . . Claudia Durastanti's genre-defying novel delivers profound insights into the connections between self, language, art, and disability."

—*Shelf Awareness* (starred review)

"Formally innovative and emotionally complex, this novel explores themes of communication, family, and belonging with exceptional insight. Durastanti, celebrated in Italy for her intelligent voice and

her hybrid perspective, speaks to all who are outside and in-between. *Strangers I Know*, in a bracing translation by Elizabeth Harris, is a stunning English-language debut."
—Jhumpa Lahiri

"Playful, looping, atmospheric, and funny, *Strangers I Know* is a singular achievement, one of those rare books that expanded my understanding of what a novel can do. Claudia Durastanti is an absolutely thrilling writer."
—Lauren Groff, author of *Matrix* and *Fates and Furies*

"Brave and deeply felt . . . Here the novel is not only a medium of illumination but also a buoy cast into the dark waters of memory, imagination, and boldly embodied questions. In other words, it is my favorite kind of writing, the kind that not only tells of the world but burrows through it, alive."
—Ocean Vuong, author of *On Earth We're Briefly Gorgeous*

"A fiercely inventive, lyrical journey into the heart, and into the cultures of America, Italy, and England. Durastanti's singular voice and the intensity of her honesty stayed with me. I've never read or heard anything like this book."
—Krys Lee, author of *Drifting House* and *How I Became a North Korean*

"Claudia Durastanti's writing is lyrical and sharp, underpinned with a searching gaze that turns the everyday into something darkly beautiful. Every page feels totally, absorbingly, alive."
—Sophie Mackintosh, author of *The Water Cure*

"A shape-shifting work straddling the boundaries of genre . . . Fans of Jenny Offill and Rachel Cusk will enjoy this unusual work of personal mythology."
—*Kirkus Reviews*

"Insightful and complex . . . An enjoyable and distinctive bildungsroman."
—*Publishers Weekly*

Strangers I Know

CLAUDIA DURASTANTI

Translated by Elizabeth Harris

RIVERHEAD BOOKS
NEW YORK

RIVERHEAD BOOKS
An imprint of Penguin Random House LLC
penguinrandomhouse.com

English translation copyright © 2022 by Elizabeth Harris
Copyright © 2019 by Claudia Durastanti
Copyright © 2019 by La nave di Teseo editore, Milan
First published in Italy as *La straniera* by La nave di Teseo, Milan, in 2019
First American edition published by Riverhead Books, 2022
Penguin Random House supports copyright. Copyright fuels creativity, encourages diverse
voices, promotes free speech, and creates a vibrant culture. Thank you for buying an
authorized edition of this book and for complying with copyright laws by not reproducing,
scanning, or distributing any part of it in any form without permission. You are supporting
writers and allowing Penguin Random House to continue to publish books for every reader.

Riverhead and the R colophon are registered trademarks of Penguin Random House LLC.

The Library of Congress has catalogued the Riverhead hardcover edition as follows:
Names: Durastanti, Claudia, 1984– author. | Harris, Elizabeth, 1963– translator.
Title: Strangers I know / Claudia Durastanti ; translated by Elizabeth Harris.
Other titles: Straniera. English
Description: First American edition. | New York : Riverhead Books, 2022. |
First published in Italy by La nave di Teseo as La straniera, Milan, 2019. |
Identifiers: LCCN 2021020452 (print) | LCCN 2021020453 (ebook) |
ISBN 9780593087947 (hardcover) | ISBN 9780593087961 (ebook)
Subjects: LCSH: Families—Fiction. | LCGFT: Novels.
Classification: LCC PQ4904.U83 S7713 2021 (print) |
LCC PQ4904.U83 (ebook) | DDC 853/.92—dc23
LC record available at https://lccn.loc.gov/2021020452
LC ebook record available at https://lccn.loc.gov/2021020453

First Riverhead hardcover edition: January 2022
First Riverhead trade paperback edition: January 2023
Riverhead trade paperback ISBN: 9780593087954

Printed in the United States of America
1st Printing

BOOK DESIGN BY MEIGHAN CAVANAUGH

This is a work of fiction. Names, characters, places, and incidents either
are the product of the author's imagination or are used fictitiously.

CONTENTS

FAMILY

TRAVELS

America

Italy

England

HEALTH

WORK & MONEY

LOVE

WHAT'S YOUR SIGN

straniera

s.f. (m.-o) 1. foreigner; alien 2. stranger;
outsider 3. enemy

FAMILY

After great pain,
a formal feeling comes.

—EMILY DICKINSON

Mythology

My mother and father met the day he tried to jump off the Sisto Bridge in Trastevere. It was a good place to jump—he was a fine swimmer, but once he hit the water, he'd be paralyzed, and the Tiber back then was already toxic and green.

My mother always walked liked it was raining, head down, shoulders hunched, especially when she was alone, but that day she stopped on the bridge, and saw a boy straddling the parapet wall. She came closer, laid her hand on his shoulder, to pull him back; maybe they scuffled. She persuaded him to calm down, breathe slowly, then they took a walk through the city, got drunk, and wound up at a hotel with stiff sheets that stank of ammonia. Before dawn, my mother put her clothes on and left. She had to get back to her boarding school and my father seemed so restless; she didn't even shake his shoulder to let him know she was going.

The next day, she stepped outside the school with her girlfriends and saw him leaning against a car, his arms crossed, and right then, she knew she was doomed. I've always envied her mystical, woeful expression when she speaks of him at that moment; I've always been jealous of that apocalypse.

That day in front of her school, my father wore tapered jeans, a blue shirt with the sleeves rolled up, and he was smoking a Marlboro Red—he smoked two packs a day.

He'd come to pick her up in front of the state institute on Via Nomentana, and that's when their life together began.

"How did he manage to find me?" she'd say. When I was little and she told me this story, she transformed my father into a mysterious wizard who could capture us anytime, anywhere, and I hugged her tight and didn't answer and wondered what it was like to be desired that way by a man.

Then I grew up and started pointing out the obvious: "There was only one school for people like you in Rome. It couldn't have been all that hard." She'd nod, then shake her head: he found her because he had to. Though their marriage ended, she never regretted pulling him off that bridge: he was deaf, like her, and their relationship held something closer, something deeper, than love.

. . .

My father and mother met the day he tried to save her from an assault in front of the Trastevere station.

He'd stopped to buy cigarettes and was about to get back in his car when he noticed the sudden, erratic movements of two thieves; they were kicking a girl, trying to yank away her purse. After he threatened them and scared them off, he stopped to help my mother and persuaded her to go back home with him to wash up. He was still living with his parents: when they saw this girl—barely out of her teens, her dark skin, her hair wet from the shower—they thought she was an orphan.

At age twenty, my mother had a wide, bawdy smile, smoker's teeth, straight black hair to her shoulders, not a good look on anyone; sometimes she pulled her hair back with a tortoiseshell barrette. She lived at boarding school but often stayed out at night; she studied sporadically. She took small jobs to supplement what her parents sent from America, but she rarely showed up to work on time.

From the day he appeared, they started going out: they spoke the same language composed of gasps and words pronounced too loudly, but it was their behavior that drew looks on the street. They shoved past people as they walked, not turning to apologize, exuding difference: he had light brown hair, full lips, aristocratic features; she barely came to his shoulder and seemed to have stepped out of some guerrilla squad.

Back then, my father would pop up out of nowhere: often, when she'd be leaving to see her family in America or disappearing for a few days, or much later, when they'd separated, and he showed up at the departures terminal at the exact right moment, or else appeared behind a glass door, or stepped off an elevator, or slammed the car door so she'd look up a moment.

She recognized him from his slouched posture, the flicker of his cigarette. He'd find her like a wounded, bleeding hunter looking for his prey, when he has no other senses to rely on and must trust his own raging instincts. My father and mother divorced in 1990. They've seen each other only a few times since, but both will start their story off by saying they saved the other's life.

Childhood

My mother was born at the end of 1956, on a farm along the Agri river, in Basilicata. During the winter my maternal grandparents usually lodged in town, not out on this half-ruined farm, but that day they were caught in an unexpected snowstorm and so my mother was born in a stall surrounded by cats and bony farm animals.

Her parents worked the fields and she spent a lot of time with her grandmothers. One of them was an *accidental American*, like me: she was born in Ohio, where her father was just passing through—we don't know anything about this nomad or perhaps mercenary soldier, only that he sparked a series of thoughtless migrations—and then she'd moved to Basilicata with her mother, turning into a reverse immigrant who abandoned the future to disintegrate into the past. (At age six I did the same: I moved from Brooklyn to a Lucanian village with more livestock than people.) In town she was treated like a mysterious stranger: though she never used her English, she always had odd products, denim clothes that didn't wear out and candles that burned for hours but never dripped. My mother's other grandmother was silent and vulnerable, her world defined by ashen ghosts in the sky, exorcisms performed with a silver spoon laid on a forehead; she walked barefoot in processions and was convinced she had special contact with the Madonna.

When I was little, my mother would take me for walks along the river near where she was born, and it was hard for me to envision this as the mythic rushing water she'd been immersed in to lower her fever from meningitis when she was four years old. As soon as they realized she had a high temperature, they ran to dip her in the river, but according to the doctors and neighbors, that impulsive remedy was useless. The infection could make her go blind, crazy, deaf, even kill her, and all the women watching over her existence, praying beside the cot where she lay twisted and lifeless, voted for deafness. It would be hard, but at least she'd see the world, and find a way to make herself understood.

My grandpa Vincenzo was short, dark, and a womanizer. When he and my grandma Maria immigrated to America in the sixties, they didn't go because they were poor—which they were—or because they needed a better job—which they did; they went because he'd chased after all the women in town, and this was painful for my grandmother. He played the accordion at weddings and parties, wore dark pants and rolled his sleeves to his elbows; not a trace of gray showed in his slicked-back hair. Theirs was an arranged marriage: they were first cousins, and sometimes, hearing the village gossip, it was this evil mixing of blood that made my uncles turn out short and my mother eventually go deaf. My grandparents may have violated the laws of proximity and been punished for it, but my mother lost her hearing because she contracted an infectious disease, and my uncles were short like many other children in Southern Italy years ago. Aristocrats and vampires paired off to mate, to preserve the species, while unscrupulous anthropologists insisted that various African tribes did so to avoid being cursed, when actually these tribes had precise codes to prevent lovers from being too close in blood; sometimes a girl couldn't even be promised to a boy with the same animal guide, and who knows, perhaps that's why love ended badly in my family, because of this meeting of irreconcilable ghosts and totems.

My grandmother was a wife right out of a peasant novel, meek while he was dazzling, no-nonsense when he was evasive. She had pale skin, a wide mouth, thin lips. As a teenager, she was infatuated with another boy, shy like her, but my grandfather was the one all the girls wanted: she had no choice. Dismissing the jealousy of others—that's the real taboo in a small town. If someone made a mean remark, she'd shake her head or else tap the person's lips; she wasn't often angry. She didn't know how to defend her daughter when they called her "the mute" or said she was a "poor thing" and God should have paid closer attention.

But truthfully, my mother could defend herself and had little tolerance for those who didn't understand her when she spoke: not long after she lost her hearing, she poured a cauldron of boiling water on a neighbor who was gossiping about her—she could tell by the woman's gestures and her pitying stare. Afterward, she stood at the window laughing, while her family secretly approved.

The only ones she got along with were her brothers and her grandmothers, who spoke in dialect, lips barely parted; their labial sounds were impossible to decipher but gesturing was natural to them and they always touched her, like my mother has always touched me. The truth is, her brothers didn't believe she was deaf, and when they played hide-and-seek and counted out loud and left her all alone in the town's alleys, they didn't mean to exclude her; they just trusted she could find her way. To them, my mother wasn't a victim—she's never been special. Even now, with all of them living their separate lives, their Italian nearly forgotten after sixty years in the US, my uncles speak to her as if she can hear them, in the funny, out-of-sync exchanges typical of splintered families.

She was a little girl brimming with energy and hostility. Her parents decided she needed discipline, so they sent her to the nuns at the boarding school for the deaf in Potenza. The teachers grew to know her by her brilliant smile; when not in her uniform, she wore a striped jersey, and she almost never carried a doll.

At the boarding school, she was taught to express herself through torture. We never kept large kitchen knives at home because they reminded her of her years in school, when the nuns of the now closed Istituto Suore Maddalena di Canossa would hold a knife on her tongue and tell her to scream, to teach her how to draw sounds from her vocal cords, or made her touch live wires and told her to scream even louder. And so my mother came to recognize the sound of her voice.

She was able to speak better than the other girls because after the meningitis she had some residual hearing that faded, then disappeared forever. At first she didn't live in a hyperbaric chamber of silence: her cochlea damage was irregular, so sounds came and went and the world was a place of nightmarish ghosts and sudden howls. She'll sometimes try to describe the terror a person feels when she's hard of hearing and suffers from constant headaches: it's like she lived with someone behind her, always trying to scare her. When we were little, my brother and I actually did this—we'd pop into a room, jumping on her back to startle her, hoping she'd laugh, but our attacks only brought on long periods of silence, and we'd regret our cruelty, though not enough to stop. The potential for ambush had transformed her body for good: it curved her back, made her unable to look people in the eye.

At boarding school, my mother learned sign language. She used it with the nuns who were her teachers; with her deaf friends; later, with my father, though he detested signing; but she never used it with the hearing. She never asked her parents or her three brothers to learn it, and she never asked her children. For me, it's not so difficult to understand why she refused to impose her private language on others—I, too, was afraid to speak up, to express myself, for a long while—sign language is theatrical, visible, and you're always exposed. You're immediately disabled. But if you're not signing, you can just be a girl who's a bit shy, a bit distracted. Reading others' lips to decipher what they were saying until her eyes and nerves were shot, speaking loudly, her accent inconsistent, she just seemed like an immigrant with bad grammar, a foreigner. Sometimes when she took the bus and the driver asked if she was from Peru or Romania, she'd nod and provide no other explanation, almost flattered by this mistake.

Along with her hearing, my mother lost other things: at boarding school, a friend, in the water.

The girls had gone with the nuns to a summer camp by the sea; they wore emerald-green swimsuits and cloth swim caps tied under their chins. One girl went out too far, was unable to scream, and so she'd spun about in a silent spiral, swirling into the sea.

It was traumatic for all the girls of the school, and the horror stories they exchanged about how they might die only grew worse: they told these tales at bedtime, these young girls who were all inadvertent dancers, always unsettled by movements and inner torments, and their stories resembled those in nineteenth-century feuilletons, complete with illustrations of pregnant, dead wives giving birth in their coffins—tabloid pieces of another era—only now there was a deaf girl who couldn't communicate and wound up buried because her heartbeat was so irregular, and when they reopened the coffin, her fingers were mangled from clawing at the wood, like Rosso Malpelo's fingers in the red sand mine. My mother told me the story of her dead friend, down to the last awful detail, and to this day, that story is the reason why she's afraid to get on an elevator alone and I'm afraid to go swimming.

My mother came home to San Martino for summer vacation until her parents went to America and left her behind, along with her older brother, who was also at boarding school in Italy. My grandparents were about to become immigrants and had to conquer another language without really speaking their own. My mother was studying at a good school; there were good reasons for her to stay in Italy. While she acted out daily, she'd also grown fond of the nuns and got high grades. Actually, my grandmother did try to take her daughter along, but when she met with the girl's teachers, they said, "If she goes, she won't learn how to speak again— is that what you want? For her to feel all alone in a strange place? Can't she come later?" And my grandmother had no answer for them, partly because she was worried about this move herself.

They left when my mother was twelve, but before going, they brought her a white dress and patent leather shoes that she was too old for. After they left, my mother became even more unpleasant, more hostile, but when I ask her if she ever felt abandoned, she says no. Her parents barely finished elementary school. They were good people, fun, a bit coarse; still, they sensed something that was key: they wouldn't be around forever and they couldn't protect her at every moment. My mother had to become independent, and so she did. My father's life would go another way.

· · ·

My father's mother was attractive, a seamstress, the daughter of a shepherd from Canale Monterano and a woman from Monteleone di Spoleto whom he met during the seasonal pasture change. She grew up in an Umbrian village with her mother and other siblings; the presence of the man of the family was irrelevant, only a summer occurrence. She always got along with her brothers but there were problems with her sisters, mistrust, jealousies.

She stole away her oldest sister's boyfriend, the man who would be my grandfather.

During the Second World War, my grandma Rufina lived with a rich family and made their clothes. She was courted by a German soldier who'd taken away her younger brother, convinced he was a communist sympathizer. My grandmother went to get him, walking to the dairy farm outside the village where he was being held: her brother wasn't a communist, he'd only been wandering around—I wasn't privileged to have any partisans in my family, just people more or less willing to concede to power. In exchange for her brother, she promised to mend the soldiers' shirts and socks. One day, the German soldier brought her a basket of laundry, and she overheard him saying: "If I having luck, returning for taking the blonde." My grandmother, in another room, head bent over her sewing, didn't blush at what he'd said. When she was young, though, her hair was auburn, and to this day, she's still offended by his mistake. My grandma Rufina hated fascists and communists alike but was friendly to the German soldiers: the young Nazis got pushed around just like everyone else, but at least they were strangers, and being killed by people you didn't know was easier.

As a young woman, she was also courted by a photographer from another town. He sent her letters through a neighbor, and she'd open the envelopes to find boring pictures of sunsets, which made her uncomfortable; she always found art annoying.

The doctor in another village often came to the parties of the rich people she worked for as a seamstress, and he asked her to dance the tango, but she was too embarrassed. My grandmother really liked this doctor, but she knew she was ignorant. She didn't read books, could barely write. She was beautiful, but how could she be the wife of a doctor? It would be awkward for him, and this was why she started seeing and then married the blacksmith instead, her older sister's former boyfriend.

She didn't feel guilty for stealing him: there was a war on, things had changed. As my grandmother liked to say, my grandfather had been "chased away from the door only to slip back in through a window," and had understood that this girl with her fancy hairdo might be vain, but she was also intensely thrifty and obsessed with money, like him.

They both had decent jobs and worked hard without complaining; when my grandmother was pregnant, she didn't even realize her water had broken—she just concentrated on working her Singer, bought secondhand on installment when she was sixteen.

They had three children. The first died, and the last, my father, was born deaf.

The aunt I never met, Wanda, only lived to be three. My grandmother was dyeing cloth in the bathtub one day, using boiling water to fix the colors, and she'd gone to the stove, or maybe to answer the door. It's a detail that changes every time she tells the story. When she returned to the bathroom, her little girl was in the tub. She changed the girl's dressings for days, used oil to moisten her withered skin, as delicate as cobwebs, with the help of relatives and neighbors; days passed, and her daughter died. In the girl's photo on the family burial niche, her skin's been touched up according to the postproduction of the period, and she has ringlets and is wearing a pale blue dress. She was already a ghost.

My grandma Rufina is not very educated and hasn't fully mastered Italian, but she does tend to be very specific when it comes to colors, relying on a nomenclature that's practically obsolete; in her world blues don't exist: sugar-paper and cornflower exist. I'll come for a visit, and she'll show me the leather gloves or the wool skirts she's spread out on the bed, and if I ask for the "brown" ones, she'll say "umber," or correct my pink with cyclamen, or distinguish periwinkle from forget-me-not; she insists it's important to use the right name for things, and all the while I'm thinking of her dead daughter, killed by color.

She claims my father wound up deaf because of a scare she had while crossing the street when she was pregnant: a car burst out of nowhere, and she was left screaming in the middle of the road. At first she pretended it wasn't true, that he could hear, and mother and son had never been so close as they were back then, both oblivious to the evidence. My grandfather didn't talk much; it had to have been someone else who trespassed on their conversations, their muffled intimacy, and made her see that they needed to consult with doctors because the child wasn't responding. After many pointless visits to clinics, their pilgrimages began: my grandparents didn't have enough money for Lourdes, but they did get Padre Pio to touch my father, who awoke the next day still deaf, with no stigmata. He wasn't particularly restless as a child; he only started to be a problem when they sent him off to study at a boarding school on Via Nomentana in Rome.

My grandmother picked him up every weekend, enduring hours on the bus from Monteleone di Spoleto to Rome, on roads winding through pine woods and past the wire-mesh fencing to protect from landslides, until there came a point when she and my grandfather decided to move to Rome, to make those visits easier. She had been one of the most beautiful girls in town, carrying herself so proudly, and yet as a mother, she'd gotten everything wrong.

In the city, she became a concierge, though it didn't suit her; she washed the stairs and kept to herself. Her husband shoed horses in Testaccio, in an area where this no longer takes place, among the ruined arches and the shops, where Rome was leather and rust, before drowning in the Tiber.

Adolescence

You don't always get to play the lead," her classmates shouted in sign language while the teacher was explaining something on the board; they were trying to get my mother's attention, kicking her chair, making her pencils fall.

She didn't look up and refused to respond, but when her classmates kept insisting, wanting to know why she always had to have the lead role in the Christmas and end-of-the-year plays, she'd repeat that she just had to—she was the best. She'd try to distract them, help them shorten their wool skirts by pulling out the hem with a pair of scissors. The boarding-school girls would walk down the halls unraveling more thread, every day showing a bit more skin, preparing to visit the boys' school, which happened about once a month. At those gatherings, my mother would often see her brother

Domenico, who was shy, a defeatist, and she'd try to find him a girlfriend. "Deaf girls are funny—they're wild," she'd tell him. He was afraid they were all like her, so he didn't try.

Her classmates were sure my mother would go for a career on the stage after she graduated—a deaf girl as an actress is so obvious, her whole life's a performance—while her teachers wanted her to consider art school. She was good at drawing, filled notebooks with headless bodies and floating eyes, but when they praised her, she shrugged: she wasn't stupid, it was easy to say she had talent, but only because she had nothing else.

The boarding school in Potenza could only provide lodging for girls up to a certain age, then they had to return to their families or transfer to a different school.

Her family was overseas, so my mother was forced to move from one boarding school to another, or to live in a house where they put up strays for money. My grandfather found her temporary lodging in Southern Italy (through a notary who served as her guardian), and he sent her a regular allowance and they often spoke on the phone. Whenever my mother felt her hatred rising for someone at her school, or a man would come into her room at night, certain she didn't know how to scream, she'd run to a phone booth and tell the operator she wanted to make a collect call, then wait for that standard long ring that signaled the call was being placed to America, the one sound she truly understood, and it would swell in concentric circles, vibrations inside her ear, then burst through her entire body, as it turned into her father's voice. She'd tell him about her days, not understanding, not hearing his responses, but able to tap into a current along the phone line, absolutely certain that anything she was saying, her father heard.

Sometimes he bought her a ticket to New York; they'd meet at JFK, and my grandfather would wince at the sight of his intelligent, wild daughter, more and more of a woman, but he'd scold her for swearing too much. The summer she was fourteen, he took her to a doctor in Manhattan he'd tracked down from a magazine article on a surgical procedure for acoustic implants to restore hearing. The doctor talked a long time with my mother, then said there was nothing he could do; my grandfather punched him in the hall. Afterward, they went to Soho to buy her a winter coat—she wanted a parka. My mother called it "So-hò." On a photo they took when they went to see the Statue of Liberty, one of them wrote, "Niù-Iore."

In America she wore shorts that showed off her brown, toned thighs; the neighbors asked about the scars on her left leg. At one of the places she stayed, a foster home, she'd jumped into a fire after some kittens stuck in the chimney that no one else would save.

Her father took her and her brothers to Coney Island, and he sat on the shore, fully dressed, watching his children— not yet American, already drifting away—as they dove into the water, watching them, making sure they didn't smash their heads on the algae-encrusted piers; while my grandma Maria knelt on a cotton sheet and poured coffee into plastic cups. She would laugh when their neighbors, who'd changed their names a while back, told her it was time to see her in a bathing suit—they'd all become Mike, or Joe, or Tony, and now the thought of their life before, in Italy, was a prickling annoyance—but my grandmother never got undressed, just like my grandfather, always sitting there in his pants and shirt, eyes fixed on the water.

He'd think about his youngest boy, who wanted money to buy a guitar; about the oldest, who barely spoke, and smoked though he didn't know how to inhale; about the best-looking of the boys, who was always on the verge of getting suspended or getting some neighbor girl pregnant; and then there was his little girl with scars on her leg, and the only thing he knew how to do for her was buy her clothes, so she'd make a good impression at those Italian schools he suspected she barely attended, though she always seemed to get good grades.

For my mother, Coney Island meant the end of summer and the boys sneaking peeks at her while she wrung out her hair, making sludge puddles in the sand, those boys, scared just to hear her jagged screams when family friends would chase her, grab her by the arms and legs and fling her into the water, certain her protests were just because she was shy. Her skin, coated in suntan oil, would be slick and bruised for days; her body was ready for confirmation, but she'd stopped believing in the sacraments since she'd been away from the nuns, and she hadn't told her parents.

Everyone went to Coney Island back then, but there are other beaches that remind me of my family.

Dead Horse Bay, a stagnant body of water, once surrounded by horse-rendering plants, garbage incinerators, and fish-oil factories. That name comes from all the horse carcasses, between 1850 and 1930, used for fertilizer and glue. Once the remnants of flesh were scraped away, the bones were boiled and the wastewater dumped back into the bay, a radioactive haze settling over the water that could turn any human being into a criminal, any criminal into a ghost. Then Dead Horse Bay took on a different role, as a landfill, muffling New York's garbage: the ground was compressed to hold the refuse and isolate any rotting material, but after a flood, and then erosion, chunks of the landfill bank started breaking off, and to this day its contents spill out onto the shore.

Glass Bottle Beach to Dead Horse Bay is filled with uprooted shoes, tins with names of defunct cleaning products, and endless broken bottles; there are probably horse bones, too, though I've never found them. I've run into couples intent on finding the strangest things they could to make dream catchers to hang in their yards, couples shoving each other, chucking their encrusted pieces of glass into the water, making fun of their own bad taste. There are boats dragged ashore that artists have repainted with messages about peace or the apocalypse, nothing else, not one inscription to a private love, and on the trees with their bark that peels to the touch, your fingers stained with chrysalis and salt, you'll find American flags hanging, the colors gone off, rusty.

It's an enchanted, solitary place, full of trash scavengers, and there's not one museum devoted to immigrants that reminds me more of my family than this glass cemetery in Brooklyn. My grandparents tried to put down roots in a marsh, and they've changed their purpose, their aspirations, every time America asked, only to find a calm of sorts in the accidental loss of objects they brought with them, objects with brand names that no longer adhered to reality or held any real value for a family that insisted on everything new, while its sad, euphoric lye rose to the surface, like a repurposed landfill.

Around age fifteen, my mother moved to Rome, and that's when she learned how to escape. The carabinieri would often find her sleeping in Villa Borghese. She sometimes went out at night, to get out of the Boccea neighborhood of her boarding school—it was more of a village back then—and she'd walk for kilometers along the mesh fencing of the ragged city, past fields of wild grass and salt marshes, searching for a park; then she'd fall asleep under the trees, lying in a fetal position, hands tucked between her thighs, back absorbing the dew, until a stranger's shoes thudded on the damp ground, announcing someone on her trail, and she'd scramble to her feet and escape again.

When she told me about her escapes (which I'd tried out for myself as a teenager, with limited success), I'd say: "You had a place to sleep, food to eat. There were people worried about you—so why'd you go?"

"I just wanted to feel free." The woods and the streets were the only places my mother ever felt safe from invisible attacks from behind.

· · ·

As a boy he tagged along while his father, Gorizio, shoed horses; the shoes removed from the animals' hooves he carried into the fields. He pounded wooden stakes into the ground, dangled the shoes on them, still dirty with dung and straw, and then he shot at them, steadily positioning his targets farther back.

My father has always felt at ease around knives, rivet guns, and pistols.

He saves sand from his seaside trips and stores it in the garage, in containers labeled by date and place; in a few cases, he's also described the contents of the sample. Sometimes he'll give me a starfish in a cellophane bag as a present, but it's always painted some tacky, fluorescent color. In a back room, he has bins of mineral chunks and shells, in the sort of box used for screws in hardware stores. I once picked up a can full of white pumice stone chips that was labeled "Moon."

For a while in grade school, I collected minerals myself; I labeled my boxes of pink quartz and pyrite with "Vulcanic Lava," "Mars," "Hawaii," and I told my classmates my father got them for me. Back then I could bring frayed, ethereal bits of cotton with me to school and announce I'd broken my window during a flight to America and caught shreds of cloud between my fingers; sometimes someone believed me. My father and I compete at telling the most majestic lie, animated by the same arrogance of getting away with it.

After middle school, his mother enrolled him in an electrician's training program. He liked mechanical operations and tracking the planets; his desks were always plastered in notebooks filled with notations about the Earth's distance from the sun and desert latitudes. His life was like a game show with knowledge broken down into simple ideas—appearing smart was easy when you rattled off data your parents were clueless about.

He knew how to saddle a horse and how to work wood, but he preferred building models and hooking various electrical systems together, altering these systems until they lit up, trying to understand how to disconnect this light, then turn it back on. And he's always appreciated color variations in a room.

His teachers told my grandmother he was too handsome to be an electrician, that he should be an actor. Rufina was proud that they'd said this, but my father refused—he didn't want to wear makeup and pretend. Summers he competed in motocross races in Monteleone di Spoleto along with his older brother and the other local boys. I'm not sure if he won because he wasn't afraid of falling and went faster than the others or if the others let him win to make him happy. He started having the same suspicions, and this frustration, this pent-up rage in his chest, brought on lightning.

His mother took him swimming in Ostia; at age fifteen, he had the elegant, toned body of a rich boy. He'd started drinking and smoking, though he didn't have friends who drank or smoke. He was silent at school; in his hometown, there were other deaf kids, but not his age, and he didn't want to hang out with them. He didn't like signing and wouldn't even do it with his parents; to get someone's attention, he'd pound the table or stomp his feet. When his relatives tried to make themselves understood through any sort of gesture, he'd slap away their hands: he wanted people to enunciate clearly so he could read their lips. He and my mother lived worlds apart but they'd adopted the same strategies for dissembling.

A while back, the ecologist Suzanne Simard demonstrated that the forest is a cooperative system with trees that "talk" to each other to exchange nutrients or release them if there's a threat: if a fire breaks out, the trees will use the mycorrhizal fungi in the subsoil, transmitting vital matter to seedlings through a dense neuronal network so the weakest plants can survive. Before I came across these theories, I thought love almost always coincided with destiny and a frightening kind of ignorance—we don't know who we'll love or why we'll need them. But when I think about the similarities between my parents, both of them isolated in the gloomy, raging afternoons of their adolescence, I have to consider the possibility that when two people meet, it's not so much predestination as a biological map revealing itself as we fall in love and discover that a primitive intelligence was governing our bodies, releasing elementary particles into the air before we ever met, passing through cities, cement walls, skin membranes, making contact with like matter and developing a form of common resistance, a defense against the world's offenses: my parents met through reverberations similar to those of a forest before a fire, and not because it was written; their future wasn't stamped with a Bible watermark or an old horoscope; it was just an unusual vibration in the air, an invisible alarm calling for survival.

As a teenager, my father discovered his preferred mode of communication: spite. He'd make knickknacks vanish, find a way to trip someone, hide his mother's scissors and sewing basket, come up behind people to scare them. We don't know where he went in his free time, but he was already having sex with older women who invited him home and taught him what they knew. Lying in bed in the early afternoon, in apartments with damask walls and orange lampshades and the well-polished picture frames that widows keep on their bedside table, my father realized he had no idea how to ask out girls his own age, girls with bodies not yet marked by renunciation.

But sooner or later, even a body that seemed so beautiful, so serviceable, would give way. The disabled (no word is truly fit or sufficient to define them) are a hidden majority: in spite of the machines and drugs and prosthetics attempting to prove death doesn't exist, nearly all of us, over time, will lose a superpower: sight, or an arm, or our memory. The inability to do things we should be able to do, the impossibility of seeing, hearing, remembering, walking—these aren't the exception, they're the destination.

Sooner or later, we all become disabled. Those girls would, too, and so would those widows who'd hooked him on sex. Compared to them, my father just came from the future.

When he went swimming, he sometimes disappeared, headed out to sea, all the weight of the water over his head, every time, pushing harder, further.

Youth

My mother celebrated her twentieth birthday sitting on the cobblestones of Piazza Navona, with a cake bought by her friends who lived on the street like her. They'd passed the hat among themselves to present her with this surprise cake on a piece of cardboard.

She hung out with runaways and other street people in the historic city center; she'd lounge around on the sidewalk, hugging them, in her leather boots and plaid shirts. Sometimes she'd show up on the piazza with red or blond hair and they all told her to go back to her normal shade of black, but she was stubborn and clung to her damaging, blazing colors. One summer she disappeared for three months, went to Greece on her own, slept in a tent, bragging how she'd made a guard smile, one of those guards in babouche slippers, forbidden to move. Among the people she hung out with back then: a prostitute who was paying for her daughter to go to a Swiss boarding school where she could ride horses; another friend was one of the first Italians to have a sex-change operation (by then her friend's parents had moved and changed their number without telling her).

I didn't know all the words my mother emphasized in her stories. Like *prostitute*—I didn't know what it meant, and so I once asked her if she could be one, too, and buy me a pony. She was getting me dressed for preschool, I was jumping on the bed and caught sight of her disheveled smile as she pulled my T-shirt over my head, one white-light Brooklyn morning. I wanted to hear her say she'd do it if she had to. I didn't know that word, I didn't know what a prostitute was, but I knew it meant sacrifice, which I felt I deserved.

"The truth is I had plenty of bourgeois friends," she'd tell us now and then, but she could only describe them as boys in dirty, worn-out jeans, who also drove sports cars, these boys who sometimes took her home to meet their parents, and she'd tell them she was all alone in the world, hoping to squeeze some money out of them, but after a while they'd grow tired of her restlessness, and my mother would be back to where she started, still clean from drugs, veins intact, with her loud, scornful laugh. They were her "suburban bourgeois" phantoms, and I always hated that she referred to them this way, because she didn't know what these words meant and because of her, I was unprepared for college in Rome and mistook a social class and an education for something else.

One day, at the airport, she met Patty Pravo when they were both waiting to board a flight to New York, and the singer pointed out that they had the same leather purse, as if this were an insult.

I interviewed Patty Pravo for a music magazine a few years back; I wanted to talk about her old glory days, about Aldo Moro, and her wardrobe, but she wanted to talk about her latest album. When I kept asking how she got through those difficult times, she let out her classic, gorgeous laugh. "In the seventies I was anathema to ultra-political broadcasters, but I wasn't on the left or the right. I didn't vote—I still don't," she admitted, and I felt a vague sense of respect for her. I've never known how to step back from my own time.

"Come and see me and I'll show you my clothes," she said before we parted ways, and I thought I just might do it, and maybe I'd mention that time my mother met her at the airport. "You remember that noisy, dark girl?" I'd ask. "What was she like? When you pointed out your two purses, did she tell you to go to hell or ask for your autograph? Did she want to know what mascara you wore or did she give you her glorious, timeless, 'who-gives-a-shit' shrug?"

My mother slipped through the cracks of the city, rippling between Piazza Navona and the Trastevere of Mario Schifano, with her silent artistic ambitions.

While she was at Fiumicino Airport being picked up by a boy she would stop talking to after her abortion, deep-sea explorers on the *Trieste II* bathyscaphe were recording a *whale fall* for the first time. When a whale falls to the bottom of the ocean, its body decomposes, releasing matter that can feed a whole colony of bacteria, sea creatures, and other organisms in a supply line lasting for decades. The whale reinvents the ocean with its death, but sometimes just getting rid of cetacean carcasses is easier, and so the carcasses are detonated: in 1970, in the town of Florence, Oregon, a beached sperm whale was blown up, its remains scattering over 240 meters. Rather than providing fuel for the ocean, regenerating matter, those cetaceans sacrificed to TNT scatter their debris, smashing through car hoods, wasted bits of cartilage flying everywhere. For me, this is when an oceanographic phenomenon is like certain periods of history: the choice between a decade of sinking or perpetual explosion; between the sorrow of an animal grown feeble, then decomposing in the depths, or having its guts blown apart in an unbearable din, a hail of lead. My mother couldn't hear the announcements of the terrorists laying claim to the politicians' bodies, couldn't hear the radio, its precise frequencies; she was an involuntary, nonautomatic girl of the seventies. No one could teach her to be something that sinks or explodes.

A close friend of hers, a French guy, had fought with his girlfriend, who then kicked him out, so he had to sleep in his car. He asked my mother what he should buy his daughter for her birthday; to this day my mother wonders if he ever managed to give her that doll, and for me, that wondering question holds all the friendship, all the empathy she could muster: she was a street child, like all those other unwanted children, doomed to vanish into the Roman night along with

the mimes, the painters, all the deformed Oliver Twist glit-
terati. At bedtime she'd tell me about these rich runaways,
about raped, fatherless girls, or others wanting a sex change
or on drugs and getting their money by selling ugly portraits
to tourists, that it was with these people that she felt free, accepted, as if all their conversations were a single bedtime story
each of them told in turn beneath the streetlamps.

She and her best friend from boarding school (unlike her, a
quiet, serious girl) moved together to a sour old lady's apartment with no bathroom—just a communal bathroom on the
landing—so before going to work they showered at Termini
station. They went to shows and readings together, carrying
a book or some random art catalog—they wanted to be part
of those groups of intellectuals, self-assured, intent. A young
guy she met one night gave her five million lire to photograph
her breasts, photo doubles for an actress who didn't want her
own breasts on-screen, but before that career could take her
places, one of her close male friends convinced her to quit; she
had a little crush on him that she never revealed.

My mother didn't dry her hair after showering and she
never used an umbrella. Back then, she said she took the bus
with Renato Curcio of the Red Brigades, but I don't know
who she saw—for her, every fact winds up as alternative history. I'm not sure if she really ran into Patty Pravo in the
airport, what she ever really understood of the Red Brigades.
We watch documentaries about that time and observe a minute of silence for her generation's dead, then I ask her if she

was scared, but she only says, "We couldn't let ourselves be scared—we had to fight," and I always wonder who "we" refers to.

That period, even with strange men lying in wait for her on trains or boys bringing her roses, saying they were directors with a part for her ("everyone who met me wound up famous"), that period was the happiest of her life—happier even than when my brother and I were born. Every moment of happiness she felt after that was restrained, confined within the borders of her sacrifices, a reflected joy she'd stored elsewhere but was still sometimes able to let shine; before she met my father, she still imagined she could be a painter or an actress on the stage or get engaged to a boy with perfect hearing, someone important, to show off to her parents; she could take adult-education classes in biology, and work in her free time. Her life, then, could still overflow its banks, and maybe that's what she was thinking about as she walked across a bridge one day in Trastevere and met

. . .

my father, isolated and bored and wanting to die.

Through the connections of his uncle, a Christian Democrat working for the Department of Agriculture, he managed to find a job at the Banca Nazionale del Lavoro. Over the holidays he traveled on his own. To Paris, Amsterdam, other cities known for their nightlife districts, where, through plain stubbornness, he made himself understood by taxi drivers, though he didn't understand the meaning of these trips. He ordered spaghetti with clam sauce or rare steak, almost never anything else, and he drew the waiter's attention by whipping his hand at the table. At nightclubs, girls felt sorry for him over his silence, until he made them shut up.

My father walked into a theater at age eighteen and stepped out again as the protagonist of *A Clockwork Orange*, though unable to hear Beethoven; the year after, he walked in and was Marlon Brando in *Last Tango in Paris*, mourning for the women he hadn't married; at age twenty-three he went to the movies and became Travis Bickle from *Taxi Driver*: every time he said, "You talkin' to me?," like De Niro—alone sometimes, too—he seemed just as crazy, though at least he could blame it on deafness.

My father sank into dark theaters and always came out different, exalted and confused, convinced these characters' actions were legitimized when he tested them out in everyday life.

As I was getting to know my father, he almost wasn't real to me: from him I learned to love the moment a movie starts seeping off the screen, washing over you, so when you leave the theater you've unwillingly crossed a threshold, and all along the silent walk home, you realize you've become something else, that you can't swap out this current girl, wounded and in love, for that innocent, ignorant girl from before, and this swelling of my imagination, this involuntary multiplying of the cells of the imagination, a constant violation of what's possible though it might cause others pain, is something I can still recognize as beautiful and significant, even if that threshold was my life and not a theater exit, and my father stepped over it endlessly, all the same. I've seen my father throw himself into the fury and mania of certain fictional characters to the point of being a piece of celluloid, burnt along the edges. Sometimes at intermission, he sucked me into his projection, but I've never really mattered. I could feel it, though: the moment when our bodies on film started softening, before going up in flames, right before disintegrating, the colors of our image brightening, at their most vibrant.

We saw some of his favorite movies again when I visited him in Rome after the divorce, though I was too young. At night, rather than sleeping alone on a cot tucked away in the side room of his apartment (full of the nice furniture he'd built himself), I'd slip into bed with him and my brother while they watched a movie about girls held hostage in a bank who then escaped with the robbers, or the one where Dobermans tore their owners apart. I'd wind up falling asleep collapsed on my brother's chest, my father growing angry when he found me like that.

At the end of our summer vacation, back home in Southern Italy, I discovered some eyelash curlers in my mother's makeup bag: after *A Clockwork Orange* and the eyelash curlers used as a torture device, I could never think of them the same way again; when I used them while putting on makeup— though I was too young for makeup—I was immediately back to that summer in Rome and that volatile life with my father. The eyelash curlers were kept in a makeup bag caked with eyeshadow and soft, criminal smears of lipstick, alongside a few rusty Bic razor blades. At age twenty, when my father was feeling sad, he'd slash his intolerable face with a razor blade. He was tired of his handsome face—what good had it done him—but the cuts were never deep enough to leave scars.

Then one day, when he was about to test his swimming skills in a disgusting, polluted river, a girl took him in her arms, and he realized he'd been searching his whole life for someone like himself. Someone not interested in facing disability with bravery or dignity, but with recklessness and oblivion.

When he wasn't with my mother or pestering her where she normally hung out, he'd be out on Piazza Navona, trying to sell cocaine that was actually chalk dust. Sometimes people caught on, would sneer and walk away; other times they tried to beat him up, but he was nimble and would defend himself, laughing, crouching, like a jack-in-the-box. One time, downtown, they came across a procession of cars escorting the prime minister and he turned their car sharply to pull in behind that fleet—and my mother wound up with a machine gun in her face through the window. The police brought them in, certain they were terrorists, and only released them when they realized that they weren't faking their deafness.

One of the few things they had in common: gambling. When my mother visited her brothers over the holidays, they'd often go to Atlantic City; meanwhile my father would hang out at various clubs in San Lorenzo—not with friends—focused on piling up some winnings. With his poker earnings, he'd buy my mother obsidian and silver bracelets—neither of them liked gold—or he'd take her to a casino in Monte Carlo or Venice. They could fast for days or only eat oysters, and they dressed elegantly for the gambling parlors, but their necks were scratched, their collars ringed with dirt; they didn't wash up in their hotel bathroom, to keep their towels soft and new so they could steal them for home. My father used collectible Dupont lighters: the way he leaned toward her to light her cigarette, his cupped hand by her cheek, protecting the flame, almost kissing her, was the most intimate gesture he could muster.

Through him, my mother learned how to slip out and avoid paying. When they slept at his parents', they never made the bed after, and they didn't know the meaning of the words "I love you," so they didn't use them.

Marriage

Every morning, she would get up and go to a branch of Agip Petroli, a glass building overlooking Laghetto dell'Eur, where she worked as a stenographer, her salary allowing her to buy camel coats and leather boots like the girls she saw in magazines. At the same time, he was at the old branch of BNL, and neither one of them bothered picking up the cigarette butts or used tissues strewn everywhere. The walls of their place sweated smoke and the furniture was covered in sticky molasses grime, the coffee tables, buried in crossword puzzles. He collected *Dylan Dog* and *Tex* comics; she read romance novels almost exclusively, her favorites set on a mountain ranch in the Rockies.

They were married in the US, on a quick visit to see my maternal grandparents; my mother wore white bell bottoms and a striped T-shirt. My father took her picture while she was waiting at a light. He told her not to move, then crossed the street: she was squinting into the sun, just barely smiling, not sure what to do with her hands. Afterward they went out for a fish dinner in Chinatown and stopped to buy some trinkets at a stand; there aren't rings or any written evidence from that day.

Back in Rome, she was soon pregnant with my brother. She'd order grilled steak and salad every day at the work cafeteria; worried over her pregnancy, she convinced herself she should always eat the same things and try not to gain any weight, though she already felt drained by her lack of friends: now that she worked at this office job that her mother-in-law found for her, she had nothing to say really to her old friends from Piazza Navona, and she couldn't introduce her respectable girlfriends from the office to my father because she was worried he'd start hitting on them.

Their life together was punctuated with cheerful conversations that before she knew it had turned to glass shards spread across the floor. He'd say anything to make her laugh, and then, when she couldn't help herself, he'd start interrogating her like the police, asking her why she'd laughed, what was so funny, going on for hours, dissecting her every move, until she fled the room, and then he'd pound the furniture or tear up her favorite books.

With money she set aside, my mother took out a loan to buy him a BMW. Instead of a down payment on a home he couldn't throw her out of, she gave him a car that disappeared after a few months. My father was sure her beggar street friends had stolen it, and he threatened to turn them in.

My mother, to survive her incoherent daily life, bought a book of tarot in an occult bookstore in downtown Rome, and she started taking notes on how to calculate the lunar phases of domestic madness. According to I Ching coins, from September to February my father was inhuman, while other months he was only unstable.

My mother found predicting misery more important than preventing it.

She didn't do anything at home, spent hours lying in bed smoking, staring up at the ceiling through the concentric circles. When he asked, she'd raise her T-shirt so he could see if her breasts had grown, and late at night she'd sit out on the balcony and drink, or write long letters to her brothers, describing Rome as a city where she'd never be alone again because at age twenty-two, she'd finally have a baby, something of her own.

With my brother's arrival, new sounds would arrive as well.

My father installed devices in the apartment to catch the baby's crying: there were already lights over the doors that flashed when someone rang the bell. He got walkie-talkies that vibrated so they could rush into the bedroom and pick up the baby.

In 1951, someone gave John Cage a book on I Ching, and the composer started using this to identify an order to the music of chance, questioning the text, then composing accordingly; but to invent new sounds, he also needed to understand the silence surrounding them. That same year he stepped into a semi-anechoic chamber at Harvard, in search of perfect silence. He heard two sounds while inside that chamber, one piercing, the other deep. He asked the engineer accompanying him to explain, and the man said the high-pitched sound was the workings of his nervous system, and the other was his blood. Cage told this story the rest of his life, in spite of the scientists who insisted it couldn't be, that this was just some romantic notion. According to composer Pauline Oliveros, it didn't matter if it was true: in that chamber, Cage experienced the foreshadowing of the stroke that would kill him, something truly tied to his nerves and blood. Somehow, he'd heard his future.

While my parents turned their apartment into a spacecraft filled with all the lights and indicators necessary to recognize my brother's crying, American artist Doug Wheeler was contemplating a series titled *Synthetic Desert* that would use optical effects to reproduce the vastness and silence of the desert.

In 2017, the New York Guggenheim reproduced a part of that series, creating a semi-anechoic chamber similar to the one John Cage visited years before, a room that felt like a deep hole. Going in, I heard my own saliva, my stomach rumbling, my eyelashes beating, but even so, it felt like I'd disappeared into the whiteness all around me. Unlike Cage, while in this room I didn't have a premonition about my future: I entered my past, with my parents, who'd always lived in a room like this one.

After my visit to the Guggenheim, I happened to walk by a poster in Brooklyn advertising a performance by Alvin Lucier, the experimental composer known for his piece recorded in 1969, *I Am Sitting in a Room*. The piece is about the composer's stutter: Lucier recorded himself reading a text out loud; then copying the tape, he recorded it again and again, theoretically, endlessly, until his voice could no longer be discerned in the room and all that remained were vibrations and hissing. With *I Am Sitting in a Room*, Lucier wasn't so much showing the physical qualities of a space as he was correcting his stutter. He was hoping the music would wipe out a defect and indeed, by the end of the piece, he's no longer someone who can't speak well; he's as incoherent as any other human being. The first time I heard this piece, I considered how art can free an individual from difference, and difference from solitude: I haven't always loved the experimental music of John Cage and his followers but in comparing this music to other types, I've learned that it is patient, that it pays attention to everything diverging from our normal sense of hearing.

In the room my mother lived in, anemia alternated with disrupted sleep and terror. One day she returned home to find all the shades down, the furniture tipped over, and open bottles everywhere; my father sat in the kitchen holding a knife—he told her they had forty-eight hours to escape to Denmark. They had to leave their jobs and move where no one could control them, to some nihilistic hippie commune. They talked it over, and she convinced him to go to Brooklyn instead, to her parents', and she quit her job. A few days later, she came to the office to collect her things, and her colleagues said she'd never find another job like this one, certainly not at a multinational oil corporation. My mother hasn't worked a day since; she arrived at her parents' in Bensonhurst with a blond baby barely able to walk and a card shark for a husband. I was born a few years later, one minute before midnight on a summer's eve, after hours of labor and an operation that risked my mother's life. My father showed up on the ward many hours later, without a bouquet and with the meter maid who'd just given him a ticket hanging on his arm. Once it was established they wouldn't use something so predictable and cliché as a reason to divorce, they decided to make up and I spent the first years of my life in an apartment filled with half-finished paintings and doors off their hinges, repainted, leading nowhere. Back then, my parents were working as artists, or so they said, but in their free time they collected welfare checks.

Sometimes, to prove her devotion, my father asked her to drink dish soap or diluted turpentine. The turpentine must have stayed in her blood, because this was when my mother became a painter. Her first drawing dates back to a few months before I was born, a moon almost smothered by penciled-in ferns. She'd soon move from pen and pencil to oil, finger-painting like a child; when I hugged her, she always stank of smoke and turpentine.

In the eighties, my father worked for a construction company. Through my uncles' ambiguous contacts, he got into the

New York State Laborers' Union, the elite East Coast union of the working-manufacturing class. His carpentry skills—comparable to his skills at poker—earned him the nickname "Mano d'oro," Golden Touch, and he soon wound up with a series of Puerto Rican assistants who'd carry his tools around at a worksite. The foreman, before having them go up on the taller buildings, would hand out carefully measured, minute doses of cocaine so they wouldn't grow nauseated, a sort of on-the-job security.

By day my father built houses; by night he wrecked marriages.

My mother barely spoke to him, and she always went out with her best friend, Lucy, a Sicilian American secretly engaged to my uncle Arthur, who was bad news. The two families were opposed to this match—Lucy was too young and my uncle was a troublemaker—but they continued to date beyond the confines of their respective homes. At my baptism, my mother asked them both to be my godparents, so they might gain legitimacy in the eyes of the church.

My mother's best friend had been Miss Brooklyn as a girl. She had a mass of curly hair, nothing like the hair on the Barbies she gave me; she worked for Alitalia and when she wasn't at the check-in counter, she was dragging my mother off to Manhattan dance clubs or to the concerts of neo-melodic singers for the feast of Santa Rosalia. Sometimes my mother didn't come home at night. The two of them would sunbathe on tar roofs without sunscreen, and they'd walk my godmother's dogs, leaving from her house full of plastic-covered furniture and its pee-bleach smell that almost made me faint. She'd flip off any guy who whistled at her in her white hot pants, and then one day she disappeared, changed her last name, and my mother still wastes time on the internet typing in Lucy's name on private-investigator sites and coming up empty.

My friend Elsa told me people can't commit suicide anymore at the Arc de Triomphe because of her aunt. After she jumped from there in the nineties, the city installed barbed wire at the top, like you'll find on top of those Manhattan skyscrapers still standing.

We were walking through the woods when she told me about her father's sister; after her suicide, several family members decided to become psychiatrists to stave off their own worries about going insane. That story surprised me: Elsa and I never have intense conversations about our families. We met as adults, when telling your own story feels more and more like repeating a horror tale where all the ghosts have disappeared.

Months later I looked up the stats on suicides from the Arc de Triomphe, hoping to find out more about her aunt from the few details I knew. I was intrigued by this story about a woman who'd changed a monument's fate, but I couldn't find out anything, and it actually looks like you can still commit suicide at that particular spot in Paris. Yet the story my friend told me is true, even if I have no proof, and I understand what this means whenever I return to Brooklyn and walk past a house or building that my father worked on, something he built that still remains, though I rarely see it now. The vertigo of evidence that's been left behind but has no relation to me, in spite of carrying my name.

Divorce

In 1989, my father crashed into a brick wall somewhere in New Jersey, hurling his Jeep against it, the same car he used for taking me on Sunday drives over the Verrazzano Bridge, soft top thrown open. He spent a few months on a psychiatric ward, in the unit for monitoring suicides; the staff eventually gave up trying to find an interpreter versed in Italian Sign Language, which, on top of everything else, my father refused to use.

My mother was the only one with the power to have him released, and she promised she would, if he signed the divorce papers.

Until recently, Muslims in India could divorce their spouses by repeating the word *talaq* (divorce) three times, but then the Indian supreme court declared this unconstitutional. Institutionalized repudiation is disappearing: we break up when we stop talking to one another; we break up, too often, from saying the same things; my parents did none of this, so how could bureaucratic language undo what was never bound by the language of love?

After the divorce, my father went back to living with his mother in Rome. My grandma Rufina also had a soft spot for toxic substances: she found herself with an exhausted, emaciated son who'd lost nearly all his hair, and to sedate him, she had him take merbromin or anything else she could find in her medicine cabinet. It was a meager attempt to kill him, not that we blamed her.

My mother, on the other hand, decided to take me and my brother to the region of Basilicata, to a town of about a thousand people, where she'd spent some vacations as a girl, though she barely knew a soul. When she arrived with us in 1990, she was thirty-four years old, had paint stains all over her clothes, hair almost in a buzz cut, and an undiagnosed addiction to alcohol, and I learned she'd divorced when I had to draw our family in class or the priests refused to give her Communion, which my brother and I participated in without much thought, driven by an innate desire for absolution.

My father would show up in Basilicata with no warning, sometimes kicking the door down, more often using me as a diplomatic mediator. And just like my mother years earlier, I'd suddenly find him in front of my school, leaning against one of his petroleum-blue Fiats that he kept getting even after a car accident—he always bought the same model as the one he'd just totaled. And I would recognize it by some removed details: the cigarette ash, the yellowing newspapers on the backseat, never putting everything together, prey only understanding itself as such when it can no longer see its surroundings, can only home in on separate details.

At our apartment he'd be bent over the kitchen table, asking my mother to pull out the shards of glass still in his skull after the Jeep accident, which he insisted the American doctors hadn't suctioned out properly. This ground glass was the reason why he always scratched his head and couldn't sleep. My mother would take a flashlight and eyebrow tweezers, stoop over him, looking for something, darkly scanning. "I never loved him," she says when she speaks of this strange solicitude, "but I was his only friend. There's no love between deaf people—it's a fantasy of the hearing. There's sex, intimacy, but not the need for love. Being alike is everything." My mother performed this same act for years; I saw them bent over, in that light beam, trying to make up for an accident. Those shards didn't exist, and they both knew it.

When he was around forty, my father tried to get into a Slovenian casino with a false ID: he'd been banned from the European casino circuit for bad behavior, so he took matters into his own hands. They put him in jail—a deaf person in a Slovenian prison in the early nineties, a short time after the country had become an independent democracy, with everything else about to collapse—until the consulate intervened; going over the court records and release papers, it's like they're lives other than his own.

When I was fourteen, I stopped asking him for presents. They were all stolen.

Sometimes, though, he'll have me sit down on a velvet stool at his desk and he'll open a series of small black boxes in front of me, like a jeweler on the Lower East Side. He'll tell me to pick one, but I don't fall for that anymore, and I never choose the ring I'd really like: if I do, he'll tell me to put it on, study my smile, look pleased, then he'll take the ring back and turn it slowly under the light before tucking it away inside its box and saying, "Next time." This is when he snaps the box shut and gives me a bunch of old stones or key chains I'll never use.

In the years following the divorce, he developed specific tastes: hand-sewn leather luggage, Acqua di Parma cologne, a count's gypsy ring on his ring finger; his favorite colors, gunmetal blue and black. I sometimes ran into him around Rome while I was out with my friends, and he'd be wearing a tailored jacket and carrying a walking stick that he didn't need, and he'd tell me he was on his way for an espresso on Via Veneto or was going to pop into Amleto, the politicians' barbershop, establishments I knew weren't interested in his business, though he always managed to get a discount.

It's a persuasive talent I tested for myself when we went to a Testaccio trattoria he hadn't set foot in for ten years, and he had me walk ahead of him like we were their special guests, though the place was packed, with not so much as a free chair. I ducked my head in embarrassment, but the chefs came out of the kitchen to greet him and tell him they never saw him anymore, but he was "still the same damn fool."

He's always driven too fast and won't wear a seat belt, accumulating a series of legendary tickets charged to his mother. Nostalgia puts him in a bad mood and he enjoys seeing a wounded animal; he has zero empathy for animals. One night during my first year at college—I'd moved to my grandmother's to study anthropology at Sapienza University—he came home after midnight and woke us all. He'd just won big at bingo. I was lying on the cot I used back then, and my father came closer, buzzed from wine and throwing money on me, and I jerked up, grabbing as much as I could. His head tilted while he laughed and rained hundred-euro bills down on me, and I was excited in spite of myself.

He's gone from 1970s Italian cars to increasingly zippy little British models, but whatever elegance they had on the lot is soon spoiled: the older he gets the odder the ornaments he stuffs into his Mini Coopers. A metal raptor for a gearshift handle, phosphorescent lights going on all over the car with the turning of the key, to the point that sitting in the passenger seat, you think you might wind up ejected out the roof; the leather upholstery is now draped in psychedelic scarves, and the effect is grotesque, anti-modern.

Like my mother's dogs that were meek at first and have grown nuts over the years: anything my parents touch adapts to their decadence; my parents are the king and queen of thaumaturgy, but they don't heal the sick or perform other miracles: their power lies in persuading any creature within reach to come undone, to slip into potential madness.

· · ·

In the years following the divorce, my mother kept walking and escaping, sometimes taking me hostage. Instead of sending me to school, in the spring she'd dress me in a tracksuit, put candy in her fanny pack, and force me to walk with her from town to town. I'd go, not holding her hand, my breathing ragged, walking through ponds in my sneakers, hoping to crush tadpoles; we'd keep going for eight hours before we turned around. She was the one who needed to be out there, not me, but I walked all the same.

Teachers were left out of it. I already knew how to read and write fairly well in Italian—I didn't need school, and though I wasn't very athletic, I liked walking alongside my mother, through the fields and streams of Val d'Agri, splashing in the still-remaining sad rivulets.

During those walks, my mother would tell me that whatever I decided to do when I grew up, I must never leave my job for a man, and that sex would be an inevitably violent experience I couldn't do without. I wasn't even ten, but I already knew about consent and rape and the countless miseries in between.

Whenever I suggested we bring an umbrella, she teased me—my cowardice was a mystery to her—and my one responsibility on our trips was that I always had to treat life like a party. On our return, walking from town to town in

Val d'Agri, people would pull up alongside us thinking we needed a ride, and they immediately decided we were poor, not out for exercise: lacking transportation in certain mountainous regions of the South can only mean you're destitute, and while everyone at school kept asking me if it was strange leaving America and finding myself somewhere so limited with more sheep than children, to me it wasn't so different from New Jersey, where my uncle Paul lived, a land of roundabouts and laconic streets and no downtown. In Basilicata, I found the same scattered American suburbs, the same urge my cousins across the ocean had, to retreat to a room, only they had no place to go other than the mall or some mind-numbing basement.

Meanwhile my mother's collection of romance novels kept growing: there weren't any bookstores nearby, but the local kiosks allowed her to purchase comic books and collect around a thousand Harlequin Mondadori titles. When she wasn't painting, she'd be shut up in her room rereading and reorganizing those books, color-coding them: pink was for romantic stories focused on resolving misunderstandings and without sex scenes; burgundy books were vaguely erotic; green was for westerns; and light blue was for those somewhere in between these last two; a gold cover meant a complex plot or a historical setting. But all the passion, contagion, marriage, and everything else within those pages left no mark at all on my mother's life.

My brother and I would lose track of her: sometimes she'd go take a walk by herself and she'd stay out, sleeping out there, walking kilometers on her own in the dark, especially if it was raining, and we got used to our anarchic life of peeled tangerines and dirty socks and hugging each other tight on the couch while watching scary movies. It was an existence devoid of schedules or too many questions: we worried she might be hurt or might not return, but we stayed put.

We may have lived off cereal and milk and those oranges, but we also had our vacations in Brooklyn, and clothes with brand names no one had heard of yet, and in spite of the difference in our ages, my brother was my best friend, the only person I wanted to be with. He was the handsomest boy I ever saw. When he started going out with girls from school, I'd wait for him, hiding in his bed, so he'd tell me what had happened, and as soon as he told me about kissing them, I'd burrow under the pillow and pretend to be embarrassed. I missed my mother when she disappeared, but she was a nebula and my father, the blackest of galaxies that neutralized any theoretical physics: my brother was the first matter I could gather around. When I'm asked who taught me to speak properly, between my immigrant grandparents and their broken language and then my parents, who couldn't know how to correct my pronunciation, I realize the first language I spoke was that of the first person I loved: the Italian of a boy six years my senior, melodic and error-free, stubbornly clung to when everyone around us had a heavy inflection, in a region where using dialect meant you belonged. A teenager's language borrowed from TV shows dubbed into Italian, still fresh, naive, and sweet, my brother's voice that still at times is mine. He taught me how to avoid the humiliation that follows from a failed communication act: the more our parents swore, the more intentionally offensive their words were, the more precise we were, convinced that a correct vocabulary would imply a correct life, free at last from their strangeness.

*   *   *

The story of a family is more like a map than a novel, and an autobiography is the summation of all the geologic ages you've passed through. Writing yourself means remembering that you were born with rage, that you were thick, steady, flowing lava before your crust hardened and cracked and allowed some sort of love to emerge, or that useless power of forgiveness came and smoothed you over, leveling out all your hollows. Rereading yourself means inventing what you've gone through, identifying each layer you're built upon: the crystals of joy or loneliness beneath, the result of some evaporated memory, everything that's been carved out, then flooded, only for you to realize that time's not healing after all: there's a breach that can't be filled. The only thing time will do is carry dust and weeds along with it, until that crevice is covered over and transformed to a different landscape, distant, almost a fairy tale, where you no longer recognize the language spoken, that might as well be Elvish. You cross the ruins of your family and realize that some words have been erased while others have been saved, some have disappeared while others will always be a part of your reverberation, until finally, you arrive at the edge of your father and your mother, after years of believing that dying or going mad was the only way to live up to them. And then you realize that everything in your blood is beckoning, and you're just the echo of a past mythology.

. . .

I once saw a man drinking noxious things like turpentine: Joaquin Phoenix, in Paul Thomas Anderson's *The Master*. In an early scene, his character is belowdecks on a battleship, and he drinks from a fuel tank, foreshadowing his inability to return to society after the war. Phoenix's character is inscrutable, easy to hate, only capable of communicating through sex, only tamable through a pseudoscientist/Hubbard-Scientology-inspired preacher who takes him into his family and congregation. When they all want nothing to do with Phoenix—he's so volatile and awful—the cult leader chastises them, saying this is exactly the man who needs their shelter. Because if they "fail" him, they'll "fail" everybody else: in English, *to fail someone* means to disappoint or fail in your duty to another. By the end of the movie, I'd nearly forgotten what happened, except those two scenes. And my only thought was, "And where is this master who didn't save my father?," and I stayed where I was in that dark theater, unable to cross over any threshold.

I see my mother more often. She'll come visit me in the city where I live, and if we get bored, we go shopping. She never wears women's clothes—maybe once a year—and when she does we stare at her, speechless, thinking about how far she could've gone if she'd only followed the rules. Her whole life she's tried to camouflage herself in sweatshirts and hunting vests, worn-out sneakers and androgynous haircuts, but they've never kept her safe.

We'll take public transportation in foreign and Italian cities, our bags stuffed full of clothes, and after years of being ashamed to gesture in her presence to make myself understood, now I speak without a voice, exaggerating labials, trying to mimic ideas that mean nothing due to my overdone choreography. I want others to see me, that it's clear that I'm no longer ashamed of her, even if it doesn't matter to her, is too late by now.

As soon as we meet at arrivals at Stansted or Gatwick, she'll study my makeup and ask when I learned how to dress like a rich girl. But if I'm not dressed up at all, then she winces and says I look like one of those barefoot and pregnant American girls who are too poor to own a TV. To make her happy, I'll ask for a cigarette, though I don't smoke and she has heart trouble. Then she brightens up and takes my arm, reinvigorated by my minor transgression. I only concede this to her in airports, the best free zone we share.

In department-store dressing rooms, I'll notice her reflection in the mirror and suddenly see Piazza Navona, the roses, those nights at dance clubs and her imitating the movements of others; I see her squandered youth, much more entertaining than my own; her consuming griefs; her strange night dreams; her fears that I'm too shy, too frightened to have a memorable life; her talent that one of these days the art world will come to recognize—it's going to happen for her, even with her moldy paintings piled in the attic (she's made up brochures of her work with list prices of over a hundred thousand euros, and she hands them out to my friends, much to my chagrin); I see the day when I ordered her to go hide behind the school instead of waiting by the front door—not because I was ashamed of her deafness but because of the black and purple paint smears on her hands that were sure to make some nasty kid call her "Michelangelo"; her fears every time I get on a plane and she doesn't know the exact departure time, information I won't give her—not wanting to be notified about earthquakes in Guatemala and the effect these might have on control towers destined to deliver me anywhere in the world, not wanting to know about those cracks in the earth because I've already got my mother, a harmonic tremor laying everything to waste. She steps out of those dressing rooms and she's shaking her head, discarding every piece of clothing that looked good on her, holding on to the one item I loathe that somehow is still the most her.

A few years back, I went dress shopping with her in London to find something formal at a large department store. Countless stores and dresses later, annoyed by her capriciousness, I asked her what she was hoping to find. She stared at me like I'd asked something truly stupid and answered: "He can't see me looking bad." My father would also be at this event: the last time they met there was blood, and since that day, we'd done everything in our power to keep them apart. I leaned back against the wall of the store, laughing, my hands full of satin and lace that she was worried would wind up wrinkled, those dresses sliding to the floor, my mother watching, extremely embarrassed.

He made her life hell, they were no longer on speaking terms, and she wanted to look nice for him? But that's how they communicated.

The day they were to see each other again, she hid behind me, among the other guests who had no idea what was going on, until he made a simple gesture. He raised his hand, beckoned her with one finger, as though still enticing a girl from school, still leaning against a car in front of the institute for the deaf on Via Nomentana, like all those years before.

My mother slowly walked over, not asking me to join her, Eurydice turning, Orpheus slipping back to the underworld. He flirted with her over her pretty dress, they laughed, she asked for two glasses of champagne; I watched, not understanding. If I hadn't intervened, I'm sure they would have wound up in a hotel room together.

The day after, she left; he cried, the mystery still unsolvable.

I don't know the essence of my parents: I know I don't have it. Any advantage I have has been lost or gained through language, one word exchanged for another, the interlocuter persuaded through the rhetoric of my feelings, and my silence is never feral. I don't have their demonic influx.

While I was trying to create order through writing, they were still in contact with the stars, with the ungovernable, always drawing me back to the suspicion that words only mean something if they're literal, and anything left over is a great waste of time and emotion: life is a silent, hypnotic seduction, and all the rest is failure.

Some phenomena are opaque, unexplainable: scientists struggle to understand why sperm whales, at certain times of the year, will beach themselves along the North Sea shores.

They might be blown up or consigned to the depths, but how they got there remains a mystery. A recent team of researchers has tied whale beachings to solar storms, charting the origin of their appearance in diagrams that at once evoke medieval demons, bestiaries, and unreliable cosmogonies printed on parchment. It's a piece of news I might share with my parents—they'd both be pleased—the suggestion of solar storms would demonstrate there's something operating in secret that only they are special enough to realize, just like any oscillation or vibration of air is enough to warn them of a change occurring in the world. I'm not convinced by this explanation, but I do wonder: how would it go, how would I be, "next time."

TRAVELS

But it is one thing to read about dragons
and another to meet them.

—URSULA K. LE GUIN

America

Women Night Warriors

When I was little, I pretty much knew how I'd die: kryptonite poisoning, toxic fumes from a nuclear power plant, forced starvation holed up in some bunker under Russian chemical attack. In my conspiracy fantasies, it was always the Russians: I was five and this was 1989 in New York. Not exactly the best year for the USSR and the Cold War, but the Soviets had done something worse than threaten the United States with their aerospace program or their fearsome Olympic gymnasts: they'd moved into my neighborhood. What's more, my mother was close friends with some of them. Strangers in leather bomber jackets, quartz-colored eyeglass frames; one of her girlfriends with an unpronounceable name who came to dinner and would suddenly grow animated, with her hacking laugh and bad lungs from that hostile, science-fictional country.

The Russians weren't the only foreigners in the neighborhood. There were the daughters of the bricklayers who worked for my uncle Arthur, doing repairs for him in the condominium complex he managed; my uncle wore cowboy boots and a mariachi mustache and had been engaged at least once to every woman in the building. The bricklayers' daughters spoke Spanish and would sometimes go with me to the top floor to find a resident named Jenny, who was forever ninety-nine and fast disappearing under her lilac robe tangled up in her walker.

My grandpa Vincenzo charged her a reduced rent in his four-story, redbrick building with a bottle-green door near Fifteenth and Ovington Avenue, a nondescript outpost between Bensonhurst and Dyker Heights, a place of senior centers, video stores, and butcher shops. He'd bought the building for his children to live in, before they declared their independence. Jenny was a widow with no relatives to care for her—they all lived in Eastern Europe. I'd bring the bricklayers' daughters up to see her because she always handed out chocolate mints and pennies. I'd save up my coins, and my grandfather would help me make penny rolls to bring to the bank and we'd come home with a bunch of dollar bills, so I could buy what I wanted at the local department stores full of flowered muumuus and Barbie videos.

I sometimes distracted myself with stealing. I'd pinch bracelets, plastic earrings for unpierced ears, and slimy goo

I'd slap on the wall. Nothing cost more than a dollar, but I was scared all the same. Not about stealing—about not getting caught. At night, I'd sleep with my grandparents in their bedroom smelling of polished wood, with a statue of Saint Francis in one corner, and I'd stay awake, waiting for the flashing red and blue lights to rouse my family, or for the police to pound on the front door, but no storekeeper ever reported me, and God knows what awful things would happen to me in the future, if the grown-ups couldn't be bothered about my correction and redemption.

My mother never worked. On those days she lay around sleeping in her robe, I'd scramble onto the bed and get her to dance or play-suffocate her with the sheets or just wear her down until she said I didn't have to go to preschool. So, instead of learning how to socialize or color, I'd walk with my mother in the oranges and burnt reds of autumn, peeking past pumpkins, into windows. My brother had told me that our parents were both stage actors pretending to be deaf to get into their parts, a sort of Stanislavski method. They only stopped this practice late at night, when I was sleeping: if I set the alarm for just the right time, I'd find them chatting away in the kitchen, praising each other on their technique. But I didn't have the patience to catch them in the act; once I raced over to my mother and kicked her, screaming, "Speak, speak," until both of us were crying. By the time my brother also told me I was adopted and our parents were secretly aliens planning to sabotage the planet, I didn't believe him anymore.

While my mother didn't work, she wasn't with me a whole lot either, so I spent part of my childhood in my grandparents' garden with its tubs of dirt and the vine hanging loosely over the pergola that got the neighbors asking how they could do this, too, though those bunches of grapes only produced a heavy, sour wine. My mother and I didn't see each other much, but we dressed alike, in cutoffs and white Reebok high-tops, hers always scuffed. As soon as my grandfather noticed mine were starting to wear out, he'd take me to Payless Shoes on Eighteenth and buy me a new pair. He concerned himself with my clothes and teeth, was the first to notice I was near-sighted, and whenever my hair was messy, he'd pull a comb out of his cotton cropped pants, the kind boys wear now at contemporary art museums, that field hands wore.

His first day in America not spent in a flophouse but as a free man, Grandpa Vincenzo lay by a window overlooking the elevated trains that kept passing all night long. He cursed the noise and swore he'd be better off back home. But the truth was that apartment was a leg up from where he'd just been, a moldy basement shared with some other relatives. It belonged to a fellow townsman from San Martino d'Agri who ran a *bìsniss* of bringing people over from Basilicata to work in his construction company and in the kitchens of Midtown, taking a chunk of their pay for himself. My grandmother's brother had been the first to escape and bring his family back above ground; my grandfather, weakened by his amphibious misery, only managed this later.

He found work as a laborer, spreading tar on rooftops, that

black pitch smelling of burnt sugar and turning to Plasticine beneath your feet in the summer. His first day, he climbed up on a building along with the other workers while my grandma Maria watched him from the street. But soon he started feeling dizzy and had to come down off the roof. She wrapped her head in a scarf and went up and took his place and started spreading tar among all those men, while he winked at the girls going by.

My grandfather would convince me to hide down in the basement with him and bottle homemade wine that he'd sell on the side; he'd make me laugh by singing Little Richard—"tutti frutti, bimbabbambaloulabimbabbamboo"—and tell me bottoms up to my little glass of mosto and Gingerella. Later I'd sit on the long table for twenty-four where we'd have our Sunday noon meal and I'd open his suitcase full of Neapolitan videocassettes. When the others were asleep, we sat on the couch and watched videos with Mario Merola or Nino D'Angelo popping up during some religious celebration or wedding that was destined to end badly, or they'd be following a couple who had broken up but then changed their minds and were chasing each other through an airport. I'd watch these overblown scenes just to make him happy: shoot-outs and communions. And while I didn't like the tarantella, he loved playing the accordion and so his friends would come over and me and my cousins would form a line and dance in the basement, bouncing off each other and the plaster walls, to a frenzy of clapping.

Men in striped polos, moccasins without socks, tinted

glasses; men in chauffeur jackets, who never trimmed their hair even if they were balding, who smelled of cigars and grape must and crumpled money, all these men blurring into one mass, with the same face from the day they married to the day they retired, and always making me break out laughing.

Like my grandfather, these men will resurface whenever I hear a song from Southern Italy, vivid apparitions in spite of these songs' implausible claims: I often fly but no one chases me through airports to prevent me from walking up a plane's steps like in the old Neapolitan tunes, no one screams for me not to go because otherwise he'll be departing this life himself, and so I think of all the lies they told me about love: it wasn't true that by walking down the aisle in a white dress and wearing a shiny crucifix around my neck I'd meet the best boy in school, a future entrepreneur or restaurateur willing to commit any crime to have me; it wasn't true that by staying a virgin and doing well in school I'd have a more lavish wedding than all the other girls, a ballroom with crystal chandeliers and drunken uncles moved to tears at just the right moment.

Not to mention that crystal chandeliers were bad luck: the day one of our neighbors—thin, blond Anna Banana—was married, a chandelier fell on top of her and her husband during their first dance; they divorced soon after. All the boys liked Anna as a girl, but when my uncles went to check her out on Facebook, they immediately closed the browser window, embarrassed they'd kissed her. And also, according to my aunts, I shouldn't fall in love with a restaurant owner and must "never marry a pizza guy": these men worked too hard, they cheated as soon as they could, and they'd hit you if they weren't turning a profit.

My grandma Maria never talked about men, unlike her sister Giuseppina, who arrived in Bensonhurst after escaping a Basilicata village as a minor—she was just sixteen when she landed at JFK.

The men of the family teased my aunt Giuseppina when she showed up for our Sunday dinners. She had two daughters and though she was chunky, she insisted on wearing leather miniskirts; she had her hair bleached and wore gold costume jewelry. My aunt—Josephine now—looked like she'd had some work done, though she hadn't: she was born with those swollen lips, and those breasts bulging out of her too-tight bras were her own. My grandparents had tried to keep an eye on her when she moved in with them as a girl, but she quickly staked out her independence, working as a butcher by day and a dancer by night. She frequented clubs where a member of the Gambino family hung out; she sometimes came home with bruises. Eventually, she stopped speaking Italian, pretending she didn't remember the words. It was her fault I thought my real name was Gloria for quite a while; at Christmas she'd hold out my gifts, shouting, "Clooooria," always emphasizing the vowels. (A mystery hovers over my name: my father insisted it was a tribute to Claudia Cardinale, my grandma Rufina was sure it was for Claudia Mori—"Claudia Cardinale was too beautiful, your father would never have given you that"— while my mother remembered reading somewhere that it was a Roman name meaning "strength." To my American cousins, it was too close to *cloudy* in English, so whenever the weather was bad, they'd tell me, "Look how *claudia* it is today, ha ha." In one of the first translations of Latin I did in high school, I discovered that "claudicante" meant "lame," and maybe it was no accident that my mother took a physical lacuna for an asset.)

Once my aunt Jo stopped with the nightclubs, she got herself hired at a luxury boutique on Eighty-Sixth in Brooklyn, but she still kept working as a butcher, to scrape some money together: for years I imagined that under her bloodied butcher jacket, she wore a sequined dress.

During those colossal noonday meals at my grandparents', she was the only one who'd get up from the table and go meet the neighborhood bag lady who returned recyclables on Sundays. My grandfather didn't understand how this exchange worked with the supermarket—what interest could ShopRite possibly have in recycling used plastic bottles?—so he'd fill her shopping cart with unopened bottles of Pepsi and 7 Up, certain she must be thirsty.

The woman wore mud-colored clothes and the lenses were chipped in her glasses; over time, she started talking to herself; when I asked around, people said her son had died in Vietnam, but Vietnam was too easy, it couldn't explain everything. I wasn't afraid of her, but every time I threw empty bottles into her cart, I ran off again without looking back, chased by the sound of those wheels dragging along the road, exposed to traffic.

I was used to wandering around by myself; if I went far enough, I'd stop smelling that perennial odor from the nearby apartments: spaghetti sauce, vinegar, and marshmallows. I'd go by the video store that was always closed, the Chinese takeout places my grandmother asked me to order chicken and broccoli from on the rare times she decided not to cook, and I'd stand and watch the metro trains rumbling overhead near the Sixty-Second Street stop, where the N line headed straight to the city.

No one took me there, to the city. For my family Manhattan was irrelevant. But I longed for it the way Dorothy did the Emerald City: all the grown-ups around me spoke of how it seduced them, ruined them, and how alone they felt there, how small beside those glass buildings, the toxic smoke rising off the manhole covers, the heavy pushcarts nearly crashing into them, all the useless wares for sale, the girls with their strange hair and their begging dogs, the headwinds over the river, the stagnant, wet garbage; but I couldn't wait to lose myself along those sidewalks glittering under the streetlights.

The biggest attraction in our area was the car wash and its enormous brushes. My father would let me stay in the car and we'd go back and forth between the bristles circling his Jeep in a deluge of water and soap. To me it was more entertaining than going to Coney Island, with its faded rides, its Cyclone that made me sick—in 1977 a man rode this shabby roller coaster for 104 hours straight (my brother could have beaten that record).

Coney Island's entire boardwalk of carcinogenic sugar was a land of foolish records and marriage proposals made on park benches, out of a lack of imagination. Along the pier there's still a ride that a friend of the family operated for over fifty years, the human slingshot, firing the public through the air. When this friend died a few years back, they buried his ashes at the base of the ride in a ceremony under a milky, cold sun. He wasn't an easy man to cry for, or to miss really; he'd spent his retirement years listening over and over to the Normandy landing on his portable radio and harassing his wife with anonymous phone calls to the retirement home where she'd fled from him, this German emigrant obsessed with Burt Lancaster, for whom marrying an Italian woman was a terrible mistake.

My brother wasn't afraid to ride that rusty roller coaster and I followed him as far as I could, before I lost sight of him beyond the metal turnstiles like those to the trains, the ones he jumped when he went out with his friends, the same friends who had a gun. To me they were only boys, their dirty socks spilling from laundry bins and their divorced fathers dating young redheads with teased hair and short skirts; other friends of his were Jewish, though not Orthodox, so they were allowed to play expensive video games and they invited my brother over to join them even if they weren't popular at school and my brother was, and how could he not be, with his Johnson & Johnson hair, his chipped teeth, and his perfect battle scars.

One day he was going way too fast on his BMX and we

found him on his back on the sidewalk in a large puddle of bright blood. I was afraid he'd be disfigured and burst out crying: his beauty was our one hope for escaping our sad, broken parents.

He was just finishing elementary school and was already lying down on the train tracks and skipping class.

Once, the police came to our door because my mother had reported him missing; he didn't show up until dinnertime. My uncles told him to knock it off—it was time to become the man of the family. I was intimidated by this secret life he led without me, I was confused, jealous, but in spite of the tricks he played on me, his breaking of the rules was also *for* me. One day he stuck gum in my hair and my mother had to cut my bangs too short with the kitchen shears; at age four I looked like one of those pale, chicken-boned punk rockers that I'd see years later on flyers at Astor Place.

In the movies I watched with my parents, the girls were always sweaty and rebellious, and as *Grease* or *The Warriors* showed, shy girls also had to be cunning to survive. I'd see them out in front of the high school after class, or on the streets at night, while my mother and I were coming back from the drugstore and they were lit up by the streetlamps: these girls would be stretched out on the hoods of cars, petroleum-blue or rust-colored Lincolns, metal caving slightly under their weight, posing like models, braless, immigrants, less and less religious. I'd keep watching them from my bedroom window while they set their beer or Coke cans in the hollow of their throat to swipe at mosquitoes, and then I'd go to sleep thinking I was destined to fall in love and become a nice Republican girl.

My grandmother started sending me out for deliveries around the neighborhood when I was five; she had me take her black bag, the kind doctors carried in *New Yorker* cartoons, which she filled with nice shredded mozzarella for the pizza she smuggled out of the restaurant where she worked, on Fifty-Fourth Street.

She didn't understand Italian very well anymore and she spoke in a dialect that was deliberately strange: she said "Bruklì" instead of *Brooklyn*, "aranò" rather than *I don't know*, "la bega" for *bag*, "porchecciapp" for *pork chops*; "a diec pezz" was *ten dollars* and "u'bridge" the tollbooth between New Jersey and New York. The truth is she knew perfectly well how to pronounce these words in English, but she refused—she liked being teased, it was her means of staking out a personality.

She was a cook along with some Puerto Rican guys who occasionally joined us on Sundays; they were tall and thin and would pull a silver coin from my ear to make me laugh. The language they spoke was gentle and strange, and they laughed at things I didn't understand. I think they really came to those meals to find a girlfriend, but the women in my family were already married or too young, and basically unhappy.

All those Italian girls, killing their fathers with their bad behavior, thinking studying was a disadvantage, even if this was the eighties. My mother couldn't change her life, not yet, but to spite her father, at least she could change blocks and move.

My grandmother's older sister, Aunt Rosa, wound up in a mental institution and immediately had a hysterectomy that was recommended by her husband, who remarried, this time a Filipino woman much older than him. She came to Sunday dinner as well, head lowered over her plate, while my uncle Giovanni, pronounced *Giùan* with a Latin cadence, would continuously shift his toupee around and talk about owning a Mercedes-Benz, which he could never afford, and he never mentioned that crazy, ungrateful wife he'd had locked up. Rich he'd never be, and that other wife would leave him, too, death preferred to his company. After retiring, he moved to Los Angeles and started having his picture taken near famous people's mansions, one hand on his walking stick, the other on his toupee, always expecting a widow to turn up.

In the afternoon, after kindergarten (the rare times I went), I'd take my grandmother's medical bag and make the rounds of the drugstores that sold Divella pasta and biscotti al finocchio; I'd clean the owners out, and they'd hand me an envelope for Maria and then give me lollipops and ask me what I wanted to be when I grew up. I'd say a fashion designer, but sometimes I'd say a war correspondent, just to impress them.

At age five I smuggled mozzarella, was Catholic, didn't think I'd ever dye my black hair, said I didn't want children, and bounced around on the knees of my acquired uncles who were always named Tony and married to women with gaudy taste in fur.

My grandfather's best friend had a bulbous lump on his right temple, a bullet from the war. The doctors couldn't remove it without causing permanent brain damage, but it wasn't clear what war Domenic was talking about, since he'd never been farther than Staten Island. Melina, his wife, always had lipstick smeared on her thin lips, never took off her fur, even at home, and reeked of talcum powder and yellowing perfume; I'd serve her coffee in a cup and saucer, which she'd set on her legs, and all she'd do was nod, though no one was asking her opinion. Like so many Italian Americans, my relatives and their friends were convinced they had dealings with the Mafia just because they sometimes paid under the table or did someone a favor.

The Fear of Recklessness
and Water

In his free time, my brother created serial killers.

These would-be murderers were a combination of the monsters from the horror movies he had me watch with him (so I could handle Wes Craven's *A Nightmare on Elm Street*, he told me pizza-faced Freddy Krueger was played by an actor the same age as our grandfather—they could be drinking buddies—which only increased my sense of the potential traps lurking in our family), along with famous criminals from news stories. That's how I convinced myself about a killer out there who was a cross between Son of Sam and the Zodiac killer, murdering his victims on their birthday. On June 8, I hid in the basement, afraid of death by horoscope, terrified I'd be kidnapped, unseen, while playing outside, so when my mother announced we were moving to Italy, in 1990, the only vivid, pulsing sensation I felt in the airport security line was the joy of getting away from that murderer. Until my brother told me serial killers can travel, that at this very moment, Chucky the killer doll might be hiding in a suitcase going down the conveyor belt. Intercontinental migration wouldn't free me from the dark; in my future wanderings between the United States and Italy, I'd also have to learn how to translate my nightmares.

I always returned for summer vacation; America was now the country of a single season.

The summer I turned ten and celebrated my birthday in Brooklyn, thankfully avoiding that serial killer, that introverted kid who'd secretly bought a gun and was coming to kill me (growing up for me would be a story of continual salvation, the constant wonder at being safe), I learned that for a short time, years earlier, my grandparents had considered adopting a teenager from Vietnam. My grandmother had grown despondent after watching a special on war orphans, but then my mother threw a jealous tantrum and they didn't go through with it.

My grandmother had a soft spot for missing girls.

One morning I woke up, came in for breakfast, and found her sitting on the couch in front of the TV, RAI International on, with her in tears and a muddle of languages. At one point she jumped up and ran to call her sister-in-law Carmela, who lived a few blocks away: she'd just watched an investigative report on the disappearance of Ylenia Carrisi. In my childish imagination, Albano and Romina's daughter was like Laura Palmer, only born in Italy. I couldn't separate their two faces; during my restless school nap time, they'd come to me, one perfectly imposed upon the other: in the foul waters of New Orleans and the streams of Twin Peaks, among jazz musicians, voodoo, enigmatic statements before a supposed suicide, a black balcony and a blond girl who vanished into nothing but sooner or later would reappear, a vestal virgin gone blue in a plastic bag.

Whenever our mothers wanted to threaten us, something I discovered in Southern Italy, they told us the man who made wigs for little girls with cancer was going to sneak in at night and cut off all our hair and we'd wake up with our heads shorn, with bristly mental-hospital hair, and we already had a premonition about our hoarse screams before the mirror; or we were lost in emptiness and didn't realize, because of a man who was sometimes a werewolf. If we weren't careful, even a father could turn into something else, like Laura Palmer's father, like my father: I belong to a generation of girls who became teenagers thinking that something like Bob might show up at night and bite us on the neck.

That day, my grandmother and Aunt Carmela kept crying, letting out long sighs, so happy that Ylenia had been found. When my grandmother hung up, I had to tell her that she'd misunderstood, that someone said he'd seen her, but there wasn't any proof and at this point nearly everyone thought she'd thrown herself into the river, that she was already dead. My grandmother's head shaking with the tic of her imminent Parkinson's, her eyes glazed, nodding that she understood, but she didn't believe me. Like my mother, I was just passing through her life by then.

I had no social life at this point, no friends left in my old neighborhood, unlike my brother, who everyone remembered, especially the girls—and so I decided to spend the months of July and August lying on my bed listening to my brother's phosphorescent yellow cassette, R.E.M.'s *Automatic for the People*. For some reason, sinking into a dimension of held-in breath, potential euthanasia, and men on the moon was comforting. In retrospect, I'd see my attachment to that music for what it was: not a frantic search for comfort but a naive fascination with death. I wasn't entirely alone in that room. A boy, Chris Chambers, sometimes came to me. I saw him for the first time in a movie set in the fifties, *Stand by Me*: a troubled family, white T-shirt, cigarette behind one ear. I couldn't have known then that I'd run into him over and over, in the hundreds of movies and books to come, until finally he'd make no impression on me at all. If Chris Chambers had shown up just a few years later, maybe in front of my school, arms folded, leaning on a borrowed car, I'd have told him exactly that: "You don't impress me," and then stern and aloof, I'd have walked away.

But when I was ten, during my mornings in front of the TV, drawn into the implausible, he and his buddies seemed to belong to a world that excluded me, a world composed of male bonding and first encounters with death, of games in the street and games in the woods, of invisible blood and viscous blood.

It was River Phoenix who played Chris Chambers in *Stand by Me* (developed from a Stephen King story), and this was only his second film. But in the summer of 1994, the fictional character interested me far more than the one of flesh and blood; otherwise I would have known that River Phoenix was already dead. At that moment of my life, though, I only had eyes for Chambers, and it felt like R.E.M. was talking about him and his friends in *Automatic for the People*. If not, then what did Michael Stipe mean in "Nightswimming" when he brought up the fear of being caught, of "recklessness and water"? Who could he be talking about if not those four loser kids walking along the rusty train tracks, going to find a body and in the process exposing themselves to the humiliation of consoling one another? And the fact that after that trip they'd almost never see each other, except maybe in pairs, but never together, not the four of them together; once broken, symmetry was impossible to re-create. One of the advantages of solitude: there's no symmetry to re-create.

If we'd been more on the ball, me in 1994 and the *Stand by Me* boys in 1959, we would have filled a time capsule with our sacred childhood objects and buried it in a manhole or under the porch of an abandoned house, to dig up years later. It wasn't about sending spaceships to the moon with Elvis photos or plaid flannel shirts so we could show posterity how epic it was growing up when we did—no *Voyager* Golden Record for us—it was just a way to be present once more to ourselves. Not that we'd necessarily succeed; you can go back to where it all began and feel something worse than a sense of loss: the slightest, malignant doubt that those photos and those flannel shirts ever belonged to you in the first place. Yet there is an old neighborhood where I'm sure I once lived, a street between Dyker and Bensonhurst where I skinned my knees and licked my nectarine wounds, and for what it's worth, those boys really did start on their journey. For me, even then, *Stand by Me* spoke of possibility and illusion: don't lose yourself, retain your superpowers, stay above the pack.

Things, for the characters in the movie and for me, would turn out different. River Phoenix would die of an overdose outside the Viper Room in Los Angeles. Chris Chambers would become a successful lawyer only to get himself killed while trying to break up a fight. For the rest of the nineties I'd betray *Automatic for the People* with other albums apparently more suited to my adolescent disquietude. My old Brooklyn neighborhood wouldn't recognize me anymore, or maybe it never belonged to me, any more than I swam in a pond at night. But thanks to Gordie Lachance, one of those boys in the movie who later became a writer—the guardian of that whole false epic of childhood—I'd understand in an unyielding, profound way that writing is just that: the stigma of the one remaining.

The summer of 1994 was also the summer of the World Cup and my irrational fear about Italy and the US eventually meeting in a match that was destined to challenge my sense of belonging. Even though the American team was awful, I painted my cheeks with stars and stripes and plopped onto my stomach on the floor and prepared myself to lose, my brother mocking me because I was cheering for such unlikely players as Tony Meola and Alexi Lalas. I'd be stopped early on in the tournament while Italy went straight to the final; our next-door neighbors had an extra ticket to the Rose Bowl in Pasadena but my grandfather had no intention of spending his money on that. As far as he was concerned, the height of glory was getting a shave from the same man who'd worked on commentator Bruno Pizzul when he was passing through New York for the first match between Italy and Ireland. I decided to come along—it was the first time I'd set foot in a barbershop, and there'd never be such a romantic place as this again: mirrors the same shade as old cologne, and pitted like some experiment gone wrong, the slow corrosion of black holes and silver nitrate. My grandfather would usually shave at home, but he couldn't resist that celebrity moment.

Outside the air was always still, feeling like one long siesta, the tricolor flags soon fading. The Chinese retailers on Eighteenth Street were selling polyester ones for a dollar, the competition displayed a batch of Roberto Baggio photos ready to frame, a blue marker smudge passed off as an autograph. Baggio would miss a penalty kick in the final against Brazil; death started coming for my family, an unwary epidemic, a summer explosion.

The Impostor

It began when my uncle Arthur found an Italian fiancée by mail. He read a lonely hearts ad in a magazine—there wasn't even a photo—and he circled the ad in red, then slipped inside a phone booth on a beach vacation.

He came and got her where she lived, in Vallette, just outside Turin, and then he brought her back to America. Daniela was blond, short, and curvaceous, and if not for all the black she wore, she would have been taken for a Playboy bunny. She didn't like me and my cousins: we were just girls, obvious babies, and her appeal was lost on us as well. Before they were even married, she got involved with the family's affairs, trying to seduce all the men, indifferent to age: she'd rest her hand on her cheek, half lying over the vast table, pretending to listen to my grandfather's stories that he was repeating for the third time after too much to drink. She'd burst out laughing, often badly timed, and from where we were hiding on the stairs, her laughter echoed like an alarm system. We stared at her in secret, unnerved by her exotic mouth and the fact that she never cooked. She'd filled their apartment with fake flowers that emitted a strong odor, and she had one obsession: Bruce Springsteen. Sometimes we'd go over there for a pajama party and find her sitting cross-legged on the couch, still in her tracksuit from that morning, and wearing a bandanna, her gummy eyes fixed on a concert marathon on the television.

Uncle Arthur enrolled her in an English class, but she was always unhappy. During those parties—my grandfather called them "parrì"—her husband would sidle up to her with a resigned grimace of desire, and she'd pull away imperceptibly; she only talked about bank deeds and inheritance laws. She always came late to Sunday dinner, and her entrance brought on static interference: my grandmother would go hide in the kitchen, my mother ran out and smoked by the gate and tried to convince my godmother Lucy to steal her brother back because that blonde from God knows where was hard to take.

Then Daniela started showing up for dinner less and less, and from the letters we got once we were back in Italy, we found out she was suddenly dropping weight, and her body was covered in spongy, reddish, irregular-shaped growths. In those letters, her Kaposi's sarcoma was called "skin cancer."

The last time I saw her was over Christmas; she was

sitting on my grandparents' couch, in a dark velvet, glittery dress—a funeral Barbie. She had thinning hair, but she'd done her face, and her lips were full, greedy, even if her voice was rasping. This woman and her disease, this evil Victorian with her graying skin beneath her foundation.

According to Daniela's surviving daughter, Francesca, her mother only learned she was sick when she became pregnant and decided not to get an abortion. In the obscene mystery of her death, in the letters that were sent, there wasn't one word of sympathy for that woman in her twenties who'd come to Brooklyn convinced she'd broken free from the isolation she'd endured at home, only to learn that her new family was even stricter than the old—my aunt Daniela wanted to live in America, her newly acquired family wanted to live in Bensonhurst—not one word about how disorienting it must have been to go to a hospital and hear from a doctor who didn't speak her language, that even if she'd distanced herself from that girl she'd been in her life before, even if she'd put all that distance between them, illness had followed.

My grandfather was the second to contract a fatal illness: cirrhosis of the liver. He'd always liked to drink and unlike practically every other man I've met, he never went on a crying jag. It's a strength that resonates with me; when I find myself with some guy who has a few and then starts waxing nostalgic, I lose all respect for him—something inside me turns unrelentingly cold.

By the time my uncle Arthur got sick, we'd stopped talking about "skin cancer," but we didn't know what to call this

other illness. His immediate family took turns accompanying him for tests, getting brochures from the nurses that explained how to live with the disease and create a less stressful
home environment. They didn't understand these brochures,
until a nurse asked one of them: "Do you all know why you're
here?" Gradually, they stopped going with him to the hospital, with the excuse of work or their own pain.

And so the stories began to proliferate about the mail-
order aunt with the past. It didn't matter if they were true:
she'd been a sex worker, a heroin addict, the girlfriend of a
drug dealer to famous singers; she knew she was sick but
didn't say anything because she wanted to meet Bruce Springsteen.

What we knew about AIDS, all of it misleading, didn't
connect with what we knew about our uncle Arthur, that he
got angry when he discovered our nails were dirty or our
clothes were stained, that gay people made him uncomfortable. But seeing him all skin and bones was enough for me as
a girl to know what illness was: an impostor, a spell that fal-
sifies blood.

Uncle Arthur still invited us for sleepovers at his place, but
when his symptoms became more obvious, I was the only one
who went. They told me to wash my silverware well, not to
touch any combs or razor blades in the bathroom, but they
didn't tell me what I should be afraid of. One evening he took
me out for ice cream. I was sitting on a wooden bench fidget-
ing with my paper cup when he told me to taste his. He leaned
over to hand me his spoon, hesitated, and I was suddenly

aware of his deflated, emaciated body, the shame behind his eyes. He was about to pull back, but I leapt forward and tasted a little, to show him I could, that I wasn't afraid.

There are gestures that feel like they don't belong to us, rash decisions that define us our entire lives, until we realize they were ours from the start, that we controlled them, owned them. They weren't accidental gestures but translations of a deeper language. If we've denied them, confused them with something alien in ourselves, it's simply because we interpreted them incorrectly: I was removed from that heroic leap toward someone sick, and the tenderness I must have felt for my uncle, the desire not to leave a person alone to his naked lunch, this all crumbles before what really drove me: it wasn't so much my desire to save someone as a longing for annihilation.

One day he took me to the top of the World Trade Center, and that was the last thing we did together. He liked tall buildings, women who could dance. He spared no expense, but when he got sick, the bank took his money to pay his hospital bills. And this was also why the building between Dyker and Bensonhurst, the one my grandfather had bought and we all lived in for a time, wound up mortgaged. Today it's falling apart, overrun with rusted cables and tools, but it's worth a million dollars: my grandfather bought it for sixty thousand, borrowing from everyone, and I doubt he paid them back. Grandpa Vincenzo used to say he worked to get sick; he worked to pay for his funeral. Four hundred people would come to my grandfather's service, far fewer to my uncle Arthur's. His disease made him unpopular.

In the end there was only a hospital phone call to me and my brother; he could barely speak, and he said he was what I'd already sensed he was for quite some time: nothing, reduced to nothing. The impostor had taken his place.

Bones of Molasses

Every year I returned, and the city was changing. The fast-food chains where I celebrated so many of my birthdays were places to pretend I'd never been. In my history books the word "capitalism" had appeared, and America had gone from something to brag about to my classmates to something shameful. I too was changing: my limbs, my bones, and then punk flared up out of nowhere.

I discovered punk the day I went with my cousin Antonella to St. Marks Place to buy a pair of platform shoes at a legendary store, now located a couple of blocks away. Before stepping down into Trash and Vaudeville, we came across some of the strangest creatures I'd ever seen: kids barely older than me, covered in scabs and sleeping piled on top of each other under a sign to a record shop. They were filthy and gorgeous.

Why didn't I cut my T-shirts off above my belly button, why on earth did I keep reading those conformist magazines, learning how to handle my split ends instead of bleaching them, burning them? The store clerk in Trash and Vaudeville had steel spikes coming out of his bald skull, and one bright green dreadlock falling to his knees. His kilt wasn't like a Scottish kilt; he was definitely naked under there. After that trip, I took my good T-shirts my grandmother had bought me and stole a pair of scissors and forgot to comb my hair. Back then a Michel Gondry video with Patricia Arquette was playing everywhere, a cover of "Like a Rolling Stone." In those four and a half minutes, a woman goes from exclusive parties and cars with tinted windows to filthy train stations and an ugly red leather jacket and bags under her eyes; the twilight of the nineties was still a slow-motion reel of people meeting a bad end.

I went back to the East Village years later to buy a seminal album that I could listen to on the return trip to Bensonhurst; at that time I carried an electric-blue CD player with me that weighed two kilos and was shaped like a frisbee. While I listened to someone singing about rain and sadness and the couches where he kissed girls who I'm sure were nothing like me, I stared out the train window, saw the island spring from the tunnel, reappearing as bridges and cables—I was a teenager enthralled by this cluster of concrete, glass, and water. That was back when I believed an album could turn me into a different person. Even today, if I'm asked about my favorite concert, I'm tempted to say it was that trip among the rooftops one August afternoon, the city smelling of candy and garbage.

I spent some of my summer vacation in the New Jersey suburbs, at the home of my mother's youngest brother, Paul, the one who used to play in a band called Magic Touch and met his wife at a disco. They both were big Bee Gees fans. Of her brothers, he was the first to leave, to abandon his parents' home.

My uncle Arthur was the one who wanted to make money; Uncle Paul is the one who did.

He was on his way back from an interview in Manhattan for a job as a computer programmer when he met an old classmate who asked him what he was doing all dressed up; this classmate was also in a suit and tie. My uncle told him about the interview, that he wasn't sure how it went, and this friend told him he'd just come from an interview at Goldman Sachs. One of the candidates hadn't shown, so Paul sprang out of the train car and headed for the offices of Goldman Sachs, where he convinced the people in human resources to give him a shot, if for no other reason than his audacity. He managed to get himself hired at the most famous investment bank on the planet, where they gave bracelets from Tiffany to the wives of their employees, especially their older employees who spent their Christmas vacation in front of their monitor. After he was hired, my uncle Paul moved to a small house in New Jersey; he and his colleagues living in identical homes with lilac carpeting and a raised pool filled with inflatable toys that gradually went into the tool shed.

Same sunglasses and pagers that made a funny lump in their pants, always leaving generous, distracted tips for the waiters, touching their daughters' faces like my father never touched mine.

In 2008, I was at a backyard barbecue of his when he dropped everything for the friend who'd given him the tip about Goldman years before: this friend needed my uncle to help him move his personal effects out of the office. He'd been laid off in a human-resources restructuring plan. Too young to retire, my uncle's friend trained to be a bus driver. His house was paid off, just some habits that had to change. In only a short time, my uncle's relief at not being fired himself took on a different nuance, anxious waiting; he'd wander around the house on his days off, eyes vacant. Long nights sifting through the résumés of younger guys working in Pune or other cities of the Indian subcontinent, guys he had to train to take his place, though no one said this outright. He even did some of the firing himself, and then after almost thirty years at Goldman Sachs, he came home one day with a box full of office memories, like those who became famous after the Lehman Brothers collapse, only there were no reporters around to take his picture.

He's the only person I've ever heard say, "America is the land of opportunity," without laughing, his expression serious and prophetic. For everyone else, this only held true on the Fourth of July, and when the drinking was over and the flags were put away, so was the choreographed optimism. Not for him: Paul truly believed that if he worked hard enough, he could buy a big house with a pool on some acreage and spend all his Christmases in Acapulco and retire early.

On vacation, he took us to casinos, with the excuse of bringing along his in-laws, who'd park themselves in front of the penny-slot machines. We went to the less luxurious casinos, designed more for families with newborns, or old paraplegics; the girls waiting on tables were covered in butterfly tattoos, and I'd sneak off and get some concoction and drink it while sitting on the pier railing, indifferent to the all-consuming hemorrhaging of money going on inside. One morning, with all the suitcases in the car and ready to go home, he started the engine and then suddenly got out again, muttering a vacant excuse; we watched him go through the revolving door and disappear into the casino. He came back an hour later—he'd lost again.

I spent a lot of time at Uncle Paul's because I was the same age as his daughter Malinda, so from childhood we were stuck inside the same box, the extended family automatically assuming we'd grow up to be best friends. My cousin was plump, gullible, and spoiled, while I was always nervous, deprived, and edgy. It was a strange combination, made all the more unlikely by adolescence.

I was still bad-tempered in glasses, while she lost weight with the help of chemical substances, and she would disappear every night, while I'd stay in and sit and read on the couch. She didn't ask me to join her and I didn't ask if I could come. The one time I did, I took some painkillers for the terminally ill along with her and her neighbors, kids with Egyptian backgrounds who'd never thought about the Middle East before Bush. When I asked my mother what it was like trying heroin—she'd only tried it once, in Villa Borghese, and it scared her—the only comparison she could come up with was sexual in nature. At that time I wouldn't have been able to tell if the sensual pleasure from that sedative was like an orgasm, as I'd never had one and was still a virgin: I remember my molasses bones and that my heart kept skipping a beat, otherwise it felt like I was an animal on its first night in a slaughterhouse, hanging upside down, the sounds and people's footsteps, growing fainter. In New Jersey I was surrounded by sleepwalkers. Everyone I knew took anxiety meds, antidepressants, high-dose medications for metabolic disorders; I'd stare at myself in the mirror and feel too alive, with too much color, a snapshot through too many filters.

After September 11, my uncle told me to stop asking questions. They knew a lot of people who'd lost someone, kids in the military who'd enlisted more because they needed a job than from any sense of duty, and I was European: to him, I was someone who had coffee in the square and thought everyone was interested in hearing my political opinions.

During one visit to the World Trade Center, my first after the towers fell, a police officer snatched a camera away from someone snapping photos of the rubble, this German guy I'd just met at a hostel. He seemed to be one of those strong, silent Central European types who'd be hired by Condé Nast to do a piece on lions and sooner or later would wind up dying a bloody death or winning a prize for the best savannah photo of the year. We'd been walking around, drinking in Irish pubs run by firemen; we wanted to fall in love but already loved other people, whose photos we'd shown each other, smiling at being so mature at age twenty and also feeling a little ashamed over this.

"Beat it—nothing to see here!" the policeman screamed before smashing the camera on the ground. The German boy was traumatized, not so much by the loss of a valuable object as those missing photographs. They would have been ugly, I'm sure, and I thought his reaction was silly—just like the policeman's—Europeans always think they're so avant-garde.

Uncle Paul's son was recruited by the navy after he finished high school. He took an entrance exam for the nuclear engineering program but will probably end up just a plain engineer, will marry the girl who's waiting for him and they'll marry young, and then he'll write letters to his wife from base; she's told me that all she hopes for in life is to travel and cook for others, then maybe retire to Texas on a subsidized pension. The epistolary novel could be reborn in boot camp, where technological devices are forbidden the first two months. Both of them are born-again Christians; they, like my uncle, talk about their dreams.

The Dump

When I was little, my relatives didn't take me to the Museum of Natural History or the Met; they took me to see rich people's houses. Family trips were pilgrimages through Dyker Heights, to see the gorgeous mansions, the women inside them like John Gotti wives or the men looking like members of the Gambino family, or else we went to Holmdel in New Jersey, where all the New York CEOs lived, the New York business elite. During that period, I went into every Manhattan skyscraper open to the public. I spent hours at the Empire State Building and Trump Tower, buying hideous trinkets my mother still holds on to—refrigerator magnets and faded key chains—and any time I tried to veer someplace more adapted to my interests as a child, I wound up directed to Fifth Avenue, so I'd learn that in this country anything was possible. Even then, Donald Trump was everywhere: he'd show up in Christmas movies and seemed like a harmless uncle, a bit of a doofus who just wanted to make you laugh.

I might have spent my childhood dreaming of being adopted by a nineteenth-century Jewish family with Central European novels lying all over the living-room rug, but the truth is my grandfather adored Rudy Giuliani until the mayor decided to clean up Midtown, and he was certain all the heroin addicts and red-light places would wind up in his neighborhood in Brooklyn. For Italian Americans, defending their own hard-won space always came before the collective good.

At my elementary school, our Italian teacher assigned us a book about an American boy who communicated telepathically every night with an Iraqi boy after the first Gulf War broke out. In the beginning, the American boy thought this vision and the sounds of an Iraqi home were just a vivid dream, while the Iraqi child was living it like some naughty ghost. Slowly, things grew more complicated as the invasions were covered more and more on TV, the fighter bombers razing Iraqi villages. The American child started turning greenish, was feverish the whole time he was experiencing the other boy's life; this Iraqi boy wound up in an underground bunker, dying from hunger, and then his whole family's wiped out. I don't remember how the story ends; I know the American boy recovers and shares his experience in class and there's no news of the other boy.

I was obsessed with that story for days—I came home and started reading it all over again.

What would have happened to me if I'd been born someplace else, someplace at war?

What would have happened if my mother hadn't moved to Italy?

Would I also have voted badly, to make America great again? Would I have spent the remainder of my thirties in a rehab center? Would my brother have wound up in jail?

To emigrate means to live with all these self-ifs and hope that none of them get the upper hand.

A long time ago, Brooklyn stopped meaning Bensonhurst, Italian American accents, the murder capital, and everyone started buying homes in Ridgewood and Bed-Stuy, my old neighborhood left to the Albanians. "It's a dumping ground, full of people you can't trust," they said about some northern sections, "but wait a few years, and it'll be worth a fortune," an infection spreading everywhere, and I've grown steadily more uncomfortable in Brooklyn, perhaps because my memories were part of that reclamation, and when I return to the places of my childhood all I see are chipped Madonnas and worn-out flags. I feel like I'm walking around in an old folks' home that the patients are fleeing. And in its own way, my family in Green-Wood cemetery, lying beside war veterans and celebrity singers, can't be trusted either.

Many of my relatives moved away, taking that semiobligatory journey for Italian Americans: born in Brooklyn, aging on Staten Island, and dying in Florida. The ones who stayed still remember the days when Brooklyn didn't mean tote bags and mom jeans, but at this point, they're too bored to discuss it.

Something of my childhood still survives in Sunset Park, among the chickens in the yards and the signs for divorce lawyers promising to rid you of your ungrateful partner for the bargain price of $350; among the boxing gyms and the bodegas where you can buy all kinds of organic potato chips. It's the way the garlands still hang off the houses though the celebration's long past; and the enormous tomato cans serving as vegetable planters; and the long beater cars: it's these things that remind me of a place where I was happy.

Flipping through family albums, I always wonder why our parents had us pose on cars, like a girl group. There we are, with our braids and crooked teeth, lying on a car hood like we're out to seduce someone. Fingers through our hair, pouty lips—and we're only four or five years old—we're saying hi and waving dollar bills, and there's always a blueberry Kool-Aid sky. Uncle Arthur's running in with a new girlfriend on his arm, someone throwing open the door and shouting, "Here's the cannoli," sneakers hanging on a wire, the neighborhood bag lady asking for empties, my brother jumping the metro turnstile and not getting caught, and all those mothers and wives with their bad perfume teaching me how to choose a dress, my grandmother upset by missing girls, me dancing the tarantella in a basement full of old men and my mother asking, "What's the music like?" and then her father grabbing hold of her hips and teaching her to dance.

There's a Hilton on Staten Island that organizes parties every Saturday night for elderly Italians who like to drink and play at being bookies. In the private rooms, it's not hard to find men in their sixties and seventies, dressed in gray, ordering ridiculously expensive bottles of wine, and inviting much younger women to come and join in. Before you get to sit at their table, you have to kiss their pinky ring; sometimes, the women in my family still go.

Italy

———◆———

The Girl Absent for
Reading in the Attic

When the sun goes down in Basilicata, the sky becomes a lung that coughs up blood, and the unsettling light makes you want to cough yourself. And before getting to the ravines, to the abandoned redbrick hotels and their infested pools near the gas stations with their lofty names, you have to pass by the oil stacks shining in the night and their red and green lasers that make you think of a prehistoric future— anything new in these parts ossifies quickly, changes to mineral, reflecting a deadened, gorgeous light—and then you have to go by a natural dam, a stretch of green water in the woods that the sun rarely finds and white smoke rises from in the morning. And it's only after the curves of the dam, in the hairpin turns of water reappearing and disappearing with the complicity of the thin, dark trees, that the landscape finally opens almost to a desert, and the burnt amber of the sun transforms to something much rarer and hypnotic.

There's a state road under the gaze of two rock spurs, and it's here that I grew up.

The first place we lived was a two-story house; the owner was the French teacher in town. As soon as I walked in, I asked what those metal hooks were in the ceiling: they were for hanging the pork, garlic, and dried peppers, but we never used them. By the time we left, there was an indelible stain on the floor from when my mother drank too much and was sick, the acids from her vomit imprinted on the tiles. The French teacher spread this story around, but we'd already found a new rental.

I came from asphalt, and in that town there was only stone.

The first day of school, I arrived in my light-up Reeboks, fuchsia nail polish, and my hair combed back, and not in uniform. Right when I sat down the teacher said I'd have to dress like the other girls tomorrow. She had me sit in the middle of the others to make me socialize with everyone, but from that moment on I became an island, mortified by my self-sufficiency, yet continually seeking the affection of others. My brother had it worse: on that first day, his math teacher ripped out his earring, and he bled all over his desk.

I learned how to read and write in Italian, but always with a margin of error that made my teachers laugh. I said "~~stiro da ferro~~" for "ferro da stiro" (meaning "clothes iron" but saying nonsense), "~~bega~~" for "busta" (meaning "bag" but again, nonsense), and when we had to describe our favorite food, I drew a hot dog but called it a "~~frankfurt~~," because that's what we bought in Brooklyn, so even with this I was wrong. My fantasizing wasn't just linguistic but also tied to class: whenever they asked us to draw our home, I'd make three bedrooms, a kitchen on to a living room, my mother's painting studio, a playroom, a workout room, and a bar. Chrome surfaces, black leather couches, plants in the corners: the teachers took my drawings and had me come to the front of the class, where I was told that rather than *The House I Want*, the assignment was *The House I Have*, with me insisting it was all true.

I could read out loud perfectly, but I'd sometimes toss in a mispronounced word anyway because I just sensed what would happen if I didn't make any mistakes: I already came from somewhere else and had no right—doing well in school would be an insult.

And so I stopped bothering with school and wound up skipping a hundred times in one year, enough days to guarantee I'd fail. The only reason I didn't was that my teachers were afraid this would hold me back forever, would condemn me to teen pregnancy or a worthless engagement. I was "the daughter of the mute"—it wouldn't be Christian not to show pity.

In the morning, I'd get my backpack, come downstairs and slam the door even if my mother couldn't hear it, then I'd slip up to the attic with the key I'd stolen. I always wore a watch, so I could get back downstairs by one forty-five, the official time to be home. Up in the attic I read Italian versions of *Mickey Mouse* and *Grimms' Fairy Tales*, and old Elèuthera and La Tartaruga volumes, anthologies of feminist writings and prison songs. There was a wonderful story by Virginia Woolf where the main character called her husband a "lap-pin," and I was convinced he'd really turned into a rabbit. And in *Letter to a Child Never Born*, when Oriana Fallaci imag-ines the main character during a trial, intent on speaking with her stillborn child, I thought that fetus was truly able to re-spond from its liquid-filled jar, and I found this very touching. I was eight, and my mother never gave me any background about what I was reading: she, like me, always thought this was nonfiction, real life.

My mother can't stand fiction. Whenever we watch some-thing, there's always a moment when she says, "But is it a true story?"—even if we're watching a horror movie—and I have to lie because if I told her it's completely made up, she'd lose interest and we'd never be able to do anything together again. Her "But is it a true story?" has plagued me forever.

To me, the book that changed everything was a Feltrinelli edition with an indigo cover. At the center of this cover was a heavily made-up blonde dressed like Marilyn Monroe and walking along a shabby street past the fire hydrants. I snapped this book up for its title, *Last Exit to Brooklyn*, because I was homesick. It was extremely vivid, like I'd been shot through with contrast dye, revealing all my insides: I may have been a kid, but it felt like I'd been to that diner, the Greeks; I could see those dumpy apartment buildings—Grandpa Vincenzo had described them to me—and I understood why Tralala was acting like a prostitute: sooner or later she'd find the right guy. When they put their cigarettes out on her, filthy and sweaty, I was there to hold her. Through Hubert Selby Jr., I also discovered the importance of the dictionary: I had to stop reading until I looked up "faggot" or "Benzedrine."

Mickey Mouse—Topolino—taught me Italian and gave me some lexical ownership; I would never have learned how to use the word "esilarante" (hilarious) or "scavezzacollo" (daredevil) otherwise; through gothic novels I was bequeathed "crepacuore" (heartbreak) and "consunzione" (consumption). And then there were those other books, my favorites, about street life.

In those years up in the attic, Fernanda Pivano became my best friend. My mother had Pivano's translations of Kerouac and Fitzgerald, and these were careless and riddled with errors, apparently, which I'd only learn in college when everyone else made fun of them; it didn't matter to me, though—I always made mistakes when I translated, and still do, because meaning doesn't take on a stable form for me, and everything I think and everything I say suffers in the migration between different countries, bleeding the same way astronauts bleed when they've spent too much time in space and come home to constant nosebleeds in the light of day, back on earth.

Pivano knew how to hang out with bad boys and not fall into their bad behavior. Even if we came from very different families, I was grateful for her ungainliness and her capacity to fall in love with everything; it made me feel less lonely, and over time I convinced myself I wanted to be like her, awkward, manipulative, and in my mind, something of a liar.

Spring came, I opened the window, climbed out of the attic, and read on the roof. That's where they found me. My math teacher and my mother were trying to knock the door down they were pounding so hard, but I didn't hear because I was reading with my Walkman on. My teacher persisted; she went and got the neighbors' keys to the attic and scrambled onto the roof tiles to come save me. I couldn't go on like that, couldn't keep covering my arms in Bic-pen tattoos— tattoos were for far more adventurous people, sailors and circus dancers.

In the end, I had to force my mother to go along with my plan; bewildered, she couldn't bear to see me cry and agreed not to send me to school, signing every excuse and letting me read what I wanted, though in bed, not on the roof.

The Girl Absent
for Health Reasons

To be clandestine requires enemies, and that enemy was my brother. After we came to Italy, he started turning ferociously, aggressively good, a goodness that was destined to reveal me in all my strangeness. I squashed that goodness like squashing bugs.

I didn't agree to the survival plan he'd come up with: to make it in that small community, he was convinced we had to do well in school, always attend Mass on Sundays, say hello to old people, be seen as little as possible with Mom, and never, ever take up smoking. He gave me a very precise speech, with all the loftiness of his fourteen years. "They've already made up their minds about us—I'm going to be a delinquent, you're going to be a slut. We have to change all that."

He scolded my mother when she signed my absence excuses, and he refused to sign them in her place, when she'd disappear for a few days. But I still couldn't stop, and would skip school at least twice a week. I'd get the keys to the attic, and I'd rehearse a scenario of what happened in class, to have a credible version of the facts; I'd spend hours reading unreturned library books, then come back inside, my heart pounding. After a while, my brother started asking my classmates if I was in school, and when he learned I wasn't, he'd stare at me with horrific contempt and tell me the story of the boy who cried wolf. I'd worn out his trust—next time I asked for help, he wouldn't be there.

"You're on your own now," he said, and for a few months that's exactly how he behaved, even when I slipped under his covers at night, sobbing, clinging to him.

It was that punishment that forced me back into the ranks of my fellow students, even though I loathed waking up every morning just so my classmates could make fun of me.

At this point, though, as Vladimir Nabokov writes in his lectures on literature, I'd discovered what literature was, and there was no turning back: I'd said that I had been chased by wolves, though it wasn't true—if I told my story well enough, they'd believe me. I'd learned how to lie, and this would go on awhile yet before those wolves tore me to pieces.

I often spent my time with two neighbor boys who no one expected much out of: they didn't do well in school and only wanted to build forts and torture animals. We'd hide in a trench behind the house and pretend to be generals with bayonets; we were convinced we could start a fire with moss-covered sticks, we smashed flowerpots with our slingshots, and all the while these two tried to teach me how to speak in dialect, but only because it was entertaining to hear my mistakes. They'd throw stones at my legs, "This is a *b'scun*," or wave a dirty napkin in my face, "*maccatur*," or stick dead lizards down my backpack, "*guard, 'na salicréc!*" and every time I tried to repeat those words like incantations that could make a creature appear from nothing—*biscuno, maccaturo, saligreca*—they'd howl with laughter. "Never mind. It's not your thing." I'd try to practice them at home—*biscun, maccaturo, salikrec*—and my brother would pinch me: no dialect, ever, was another rule.

Dialect was a challenge for me and for my mother—she couldn't read our neighbors' bilabials and would only pretend she understood. People didn't notice and just kept talking, but I knew she was nodding to be polite or else because she was tired. She didn't want me to step in and interpret; I'd explain what the teachers said at the school's parent-teacher conferences only after we got home. In town there was a strange resistance to my mother's deafness: someone called her "*a' mercan*"—the American—but those in the older generation called her "the mute," though she actually talked too much and wasn't the least bit shy. No one ever called her "the deaf woman."

Everybody in town had a nickname—that's the one rule I would have added to my brother's list if I could, that we needed to get ourselves a decent nickname, otherwise we were just the foreigners—but it was disconcerting to be thought of as the daughter of someone who couldn't speak—it was more offensive to me than the fact that they mislabeled her. As if they were telling me my mother didn't have a disability—she was stupid.

Then those old folks started dying off, and even that title disappeared, as did the tendency to address children playing outside with the patriarchal "Who do you belong to?" now replaced by the more respectable "Whose daughter are you?" but I was just as embarrassed to respond to this and eventually would identify myself by where I lived, "the tallest house in town, at the bend in the road."

Instead of sleeping, my mother consulted tarot cards at night, and when we walked through the areas devoured by the 1980 earthquake, searching for artifacts in the lichen-covered rubble of collapsed houses, she'd tell me witches once lived there; she'd gather Spanish broom and snakeskins and carry them home; traces of chicken blood on the ground meant an evil sacrifice performed against her, and there was no persuading her that nature wasn't made up of signs but rather, deceptions.

One of my favorite games to play with my friends was hunting for fossils in an abandoned cave and pretending they were evidence of a lost civilization: a virgin girl left these teeth from a comb for her betrothed after he died; a pottery shard came from the baron's vase; searching through caves we found ledgers full of figures, and we decided these were the diaries of an assassin or a wizard; we'd pass them back and forth and tell each other their stories, until the sun dropped low and the boys' mothers were shouting for them to come home. There was something in the ambience of that town that made me believe a little in my mother's visions. I'd think this as I watched local herders home from the pastures slipping their hands into the flames in the fireplace and never getting burned.

Right when I first started in school I was warned about a local man, an old hunchback who turned into a werewolf: during the August patronal festivals, I always came home after midnight and had to walk by his house, and I couldn't help but peek through his windows, almost hoping he'd come creeping down along the wall and bare his yellow fangs.

My father let me watch *Bram Stoker's Dracula*, though it wasn't suitable for kids my age; I'd whined until he bought me the pirated video at a market stall over Christmas vacation. Soon after watching that Francis Ford Coppola movie, I started writing stories filled with girls old enough to marry who were disobedient, corruptible, pale like Winona Ryder. And that's how I had to be, corruptible, for the boy from school who asked me to bring my video over for us to watch, with the excuse of doing our homework. His mother came in right when these vampy female vampires were about to attack poor Jonathan Harker. She started screaming, insisting we watch a documentary on dolphins so we'd forget those red-eyed vampires, but it was too late. I thought that boy was nice—he'd been the first at school to talk to me, to offer me a cookie and break my spell of isolation and loneliness.

There was a guy who swore that over the winter, he was near the bridge dividing the old side of town from the new when, through a veil of mist, a white horse came careening wildly, then plunged over the bridge, but no remains were ever found; I never unearthed the corpse of Ichabod Crane, dead by suicide, with the tip of my shoe. But my favorite was the ship's engineer, who was so smart he went mad, or maybe it was because of a mysterious woman who abandoned him and left for Argentina. He returned to his parents' house, grew his white hair long, and wandered the town in his blue over-coat, the greatest ghost of all.

The Girl Absent
for Family Concerns

In fifth grade I was kidnapped. By my father. We took a long trip through Central Italy, between Abruzzo and Molise, to places I haven't seen since; we slept in three-star hotels and I always asked at the desk for two single beds. He'd picked me up at school to take me to lunch, and I only realized we weren't in Basilicata anymore when we reached the yellow, factory-filled plains. His mission objective was to meet with my mother, in exchange for me, but he couldn't speak to her to tell her this, so we'd stop at Autogrill stations and look for a pay phone. He'd pass me tokens and I'd ask the lady living on the floor above us to have my mother and brother come up, to sign the terms of my ransom; we didn't have a landline.

My mother didn't want to know anything about it; I admired her at first for not giving in to her ex-husband's threats, but as the week wore on, I grew increasingly impatient: I was tired of eating steak and pizza in restaurants with damask tablecloths, surrounded by lonely men; was tired of watching my father as he mimed his demands and then kicked at the red plastic side of the SIP phone booth while I beat my forehead against the glass.

To break the boredom, one day I tried to open the car door and leap out onto a slow-moving road in Abruzzo; my father grabbed me by the scruff of the neck and for a little while, he called a truce with me over those phone calls.

There was still snow in places, and I had no coat—I was wearing my same clothes from school, a green wool sweater, wide, beige Charlie Chaplin pants, and a pair of black lace-up shoes that my brother picked out because he liked girls who dressed like boys and I wanted to be what he wanted. I insisted my father at least buy me some pajamas; as soon as he fell asleep, I'd try to take his keys from his pockets or steal his money. I sometimes thought about going downstairs and saying I wasn't his daughter, or else watering down the wine at dinner.

I actually did that once, but when he came back from the bathroom and took a sip from his glass, his mouth twisted into a sadistic sneer, and he ordered another bottle. We'd leave again in the middle of the night with me clinging to the cardoor handle, lock down, hoping sooner or later the swerving would end, that we wouldn't wind up lying dead on a steep hillside, beside old washing machines and nosed by foxes.

I had my hair cut in a pageboy, with bangs, because that's how I liked it, Natalie Portman–style in *Léon*, another movie my father loved. Back then he was convinced he was a mercenary soldier and would open the glove box and show me his collection of knives with inlaid teak and mother-of-pearl handles.

In a seafood restaurant in Salerno with shining floors and a white-lacquer piano where a bon vivant sat playing "Onda su Onda" over and over, he was working at cracking open my lobster, when he laid down his knife and said, "All right, I'll take you home," even though my mother still refused to see him. The night before, at dinner, I'd looked at him and said, "Dad, enough," with an expression I'd wear many times as an adult, sitting across from friends in cafés while they talked about feeling stuck and unhappy, and my stomach clenching with nausea, and my urge to look away.

The truth is there was something my mother wanted from my father, but it wasn't me: it was a silver bracelet with obsidian stones that he'd stolen from her before the divorce. I started to eat my lobster, flooded with relief—I couldn't wait to see my brother again—and then my father dug in his pocket, pulled out a velvet case, and showed me the bracelet he'd brought along. "She's not getting this back," he scoffed, and I hoped this nasty little trick wouldn't upset her.

My kidnapping had a basic function: it made me realize I was shrewder than my parents, and that I was no longer a child. I couldn't wash up with the bathroom door open, I had to change by myself, and I couldn't sleep in the same bed with a male, even if he was family. It made me realize—in spite of all my efforts and my brother's list of rules—that I wasn't normal. My math teacher, the same lady who'd come to save me on the roof, explained this carefully the day I returned to class, when I was still an island at my desk in the middle of the room, with stagnant water all around. After she'd spoken with the carabinieri in the hall, she slammed the door and said exactly that: "It's not normal to be kidnapped by a parent. It's not normal to go out on the roof and read. It's not normal to go out walking in the rain from town to town," and she sounded so severe that my classmates were appalled, not only out of solidarity with me but because it got them thinking about all the ways that they weren't normal, or their families might not be.

And so I started going to school more often, until I was going every day, and I learned not to mispronounce things; I let go of the urge to learn dialect.

The solution my teachers came up with after my kidnapping and other instances of obvious social marginalization (my brother and I grew extremely well behaved around social workers) was to give me the female lead in the Christmas pageant.

In the Christmas pageant, I would play the Madonna, and the role of Joseph would go to the boy with the best grades. This announcement drew panic among the girls in my class, who started crying and complaining to their parents. But all this hysteria ended the moment the teachers explained that this would be a special Nativity: Mary and Joseph were actually Moroccan immigrants who arrived in town after a long journey. Mary was about to bring Jesus into the world, and as the play went on, the suspicious townspeople would discover a sense of sympathy in themselves that they didn't realize was possible, as they took Mary and Joseph in.

The morning of the performance, I stayed in the classroom with the boy playing Joseph so we could put on our robes, and then someone applied brown powder to his face. When it was my turn, the teacher who'd tucked a fake belly under my sweater now studied me and set the powder aside. "You're already dark enough," she said, though in the photos that came out weeks after the recital I thought I looked ill.

Distant like Mary, and timid like a stowaway.

The Girl Absent
for Dizzy Spells

A childhood peppered with dead animals.

We were still living in America when our father bought a Russian tortoise, destined to reign over the living room, obnoxious and despised by all. Because of how it reacted to the tortoises my brother and I had received as a party favor. One day the Russian tortoise chopped off the others' heads; my brother and I sat contemplating those nearly empty shells for an entire afternoon. Then there were the hedgehogs picked up by the road that suffocated in shoeboxes, the snails forgotten in airtight plastic containers and left to melt in the sun.

I don't know when I lost my sense of religion, when I laid aside the fantasy of dying on an altar immersed in roses and thorns like a Spanish saint, but I do know that in elementary school, one night before Easter, the priest decided to give chicks to all the children of the parish church. The chicks were in little paper cages with a tuft of straw on the floor, and I was thrilled to bring mine home, though all my previous efforts at owning pets had ended badly. The next morning, my brother and my mother told me to take a look at the bird—it had to go, was spitting blood, feathers stained, little beak encrusted in black. I thought I hadn't taken proper care of my chick, but it happened to all the other chicks as well, a mysterious nocturnal epidemic that made all of us children wake up on Easter morning with something to bury, our hands smeared with mucus and feathers. That scene had an underlying influence on me, inspiring the collapse of any spiritual instinct I possessed.

Like my mother, I also went to a summer camp once, but I didn't lose a friend in the sea. We had no car and couldn't afford a trip to the Ionian Sea, so when my mother told me I'd be going there for a month of summer camp, I thought she was crazy. She'd learned about the camp from the father of my best friend at the time, the cutest, shyest girl in town. He was a male nurse at the public health care facility where we also went to see our social workers. I met him on the street and immediately asked if his daughter would be going, too, that I couldn't wait. He said, "No, she's not going," and I'd have to figure out why on my own: it was a camp in a brutalist-style apartment complex, and it was for underprivileged children.

I arrived the first day with my travel bag, crossed over the threshold, shook hands with the female counselors, saying, "It's a pleasure." I looked hard in their eyes so they'd understand that my being there was a mistake: I was educated, my unfortunate circumstances were only temporary. And here I was surrounded by girls in two-piece swimsuits, eight-year-olds discussing cigarettes, doing somersaults and strange cartwheels, arching their backs, twisting until they looked like the whips men in town used on oxen and sometimes also to beat their daughters, my classmates. I slept in the girls' dormitory, in my one pair of pajamas, hoping no one would steal anything from my locker.

One morning I rolled over onto my stomach and saw a skinny boy reading *The Paul Street Boys*. With the desperate optimism of someone who's glimpsed a way out, I told him I liked reading, too—Stephen King, comic books, *Cuore*—he sat up and crossed his legs and told me about the sad death of Private Nemecsek, who had water on the lungs, a death right out of *Alien*. Even with that spoiler, I asked if I could borrow the book and then I did something for the first time that would become a future habit: I lied about reading the entire book. I wanted to return it to him the next day, to show him I'd stayed up all night, so I read the most important parts and skipped the rest, and the next morning, faced with this incredibly fast reader, it was clear that we should be boyfriend and girlfriend. He was from Campania, gaunt, with a hooked nose—even when I was little I knew what I liked. Then came a thin girl in a two-piece suit to disrupt my calm, my relationship composed of books and ice cream and an absence of kisses.

They'd met while I was busy with my group activities; she'd just arrived. She was already starting to develop, was tough, wore her ash-blond hair in a long ponytail riddled with split ends. And she had her troubles: she came from a family with a history of fighting and drug addiction, and there was a chance that she and her little sister might wind up in foster care; all her stories were a *via crucis* of masterful scenes—prison, molesting uncles, and foster families—and I felt a knot of pain in my stomach, I was livid, there on the shore, thinking they'd taken this from me as well, the privilege of incomparable suffering. What point was there to my family story if I couldn't blackmail people with my tragedy?

This girl had suffered more than me; I couldn't compete with her various abandonments. Even my parents' story felt run-of-the-mill before this epic of guns and jail—mine seemed more like a trauma of losers—my parents' disability had stamped out all their desire, something you understand even as a child. This boy from Campania, at a fair one night, told me that he didn't know how to choose. That this other girl needed a boyfriend, that she was weaker, I was stronger. He didn't say that she was thin and I wasn't, that she was blond and I wasn't; he didn't say that I wanted to talk about books and she wanted her thighs stroked: he said she needed to be loved more, and I was stunned and stared at him under the bumper-car lights before he walked off to buy a Popsicle. He said he hadn't decided yet. But it was all over.

Then that girl came and sat down beside me on the low wall and told me not to get too worked up about it, that one day I'd find a love proportionate to my problems: all I did was lie about my origins, cut my fruit with a fork and knife like my father was an Oxford tutor, and here she was instead confessing all her morbid secrets, vomiting up salt water and suffering at every stroke, doing this even with me, her rival. She had no shame.

After Coney Island, that was the first fair of my life, and also the saddest, with a pop hit playing in the background that might pertain to other people's enjoyment but definitely not mine: the typical disco song I'd always hear while waiting in line at a bar, when my attention was at a low ebb, frustrated by this summer ritual shared with people of a different ilk, no doubt inferior, with whom I had absolutely no interest in plumbing the hedonistic depths. When in the background, something like "Missing" by Everything but the Girl might come on, and I'd be frozen in the bumper-car line, in front of the boy working the rides, the bearer of a troubling exoticism: Why did he return every summer, his eyes always meaner, his clothes always worse?

I just kept sitting on that low wall by the rides enduring my first defeat in love, hoping it might happen to me, too, that my lungs might fill up with water.

The Girl Absent
for Heartbreak

And then my body came to me. My friends and I would race home from school hoping we'd bleed, inventing a mishmash of symptoms—palpitations in the lower belly, nausea, an urge for chocolate—like what we heard pregnant women complain about on television. We were certain that the more we talked about it, the sooner it would come, and we laid bets while we ate our afternoon snacks about who would be first. I figured I'd be close to last. But I was third, which I proudly announced one February morning. It was only then that my girlfriends started to change their minds about me: my whole family might have problems, but biology was on my side. I bled like any other girl.

In the spring, when afternoon classes were over, we'd go

watch the soccer matches out on the athletic field, and we'd
wait for someone to dedicate a goal to us. We hoped the boy we
liked just then—it never lasted more than a couple of weeks—
would step back from the net and give us a sign, point in
our direction, stopping below the cement steps we were all
squeezed onto together. Those cold, sunny days at the end of
April, avoiding jackets to show off our breasts, and insisting,
"I am not shivering," when grown-ups pointed out our goose
bumps; Saturday nights, our first forays into drinking, flat,
cheap, German beer, usually at my place, ready to stop at the
rare rumbling of a motorcycle.

Val d'Agri was along the route for some motorcycle rallies,
but bikers rarely rode up to my town—there wasn't much
to see. It was just a village, one simple church and bars that
kept reopening then shutting down again because a competi-
tor would report them to the authorities; their main revenue
came from slot machines. We heard the rumble of motor-
cycles and squealed like telephones; one girl turned out the
light and I rolled down the shutters; then we hid in the bathroom to spy on the bikers, certain they were going to pull up
right outside the house. When they disappeared around the
curve, our terror of being ravaged soon dwindled to disappointment, and we stayed where we were, hoping to hear
them return.

My mother came down from the attic where she retreated
to paint, and she found us in all our hysterical excitement,
frantically waving our hands, signaling for her to turn off the
light, and when we told her we were frightened of the motor-

cyclists, she had to trust what our expressions and laughter were saying instead, that we weren't frightened but something else. "I'll handle it," she said and went outside with the dog for a cigarette, sitting on the low wall, waiting for them to come by again. There were maybe eight of them, including a woman, some of them middle-aged and pudgy, others brawny but definitely not tempting.

I hated my mother for making them remove their helmets and then asking for a cigarette; I hated her for shattering that mystery when there were so few for me and my friends to exploit.

At school, in town, even at the high school of the larger town nearby, everything was already revealed: everyone knew who we "belonged to," how much our parents made—if they made anything—what grades we had in Italian and math, or if we got too drunk at a party once; everyone knew if we kissed with tongue or not, if we'd let you go over or under our shirt, and when we'd be getting ready for New Year's parties or celebrating someone's eighteenth birthday; it didn't matter how much makeup we put on or how unpredictable our dresses were, because right when we stepped through the door, all the stage smoke melted away, there was never a new guy to talk to, we could only fall in love out of habit, our childhood friends recycled as lovers, and then in a turn of fortune, we'd go from being the little match girl to the most popular, most beautiful girl of the moment—but it only lasted a few weeks.

In tenth grade, a teacher was back after having a nervous

breakdown; she looked like Hope Sandoval from Mazzy Star. She taught Italian and geography.

She walked into class dressed like a nun just escaped from a nunnery, with black circles under her eyes and toffee freckles. Around that time, we were going through a rather foggy religious phase due to the best student in school, who'd stopped listening to grunge to devote himself to Saint Augustine. He'd lost twelve kilos over the summer, read *The Confessions*, and wandered around in sandals even when it was cold out; for a while he got us to believe that the Holy Spirit was more controversial than anything we'd ever experienced. The class was already swarming with girls who attended charismatic rallies where they'd speak in tongues, their eyes rolling back, benign, sensual jolts passing through them like eels.

My peers everywhere were losing friends to drugs; I was losing them to Jesus Christ.

Our teacher announced she wasn't going to use our textbooks—she'd teach us Dante and Petrarch as college units, and each of us would also take a turn at teaching. When she was younger, she briefly participated in a famous avant-garde theater company; during an internship, she fell in love with one of the permanent members, and her heart was still broken. How was it even possible that a woman with such an adventurous life had wound up teaching at a no-name high school built on some kind of company parking lot, and was about to initiate us into the performing arts as a tribute to her former love? I couldn't begin to explain it.

One day she took us hostage in the gym and told us we'd be working on a political S and M performance piece, trying to identify our generation's Vietnam. We had to free ourselves, experience rapture and war and let out any obscenity that came to mind. Pretty quickly we stopped laughing and even the shyest girls in class were collapsing to the gym floor, exorcising their private frustrations. We'd formed a column, were pounding on the floor like soldiers, when I opened my eyes and saw the other two hundred students in school and the entire faculty staring back at us, mouths hanging open.

We were questioned about the meaning of this activity, if we'd been forced, if we thought our teacher was perhaps not quite right in the head.

One girl said that in geography, our teacher had made us memorize all the African capitals, because we couldn't go out in the world without being curious and respectful of others, and the phys ed teacher commented: "What—like Africans know where Basilicata is?"

After that time in the gym, the French teacher took me aside and said: "She's a good person in need of God. Keep her company. Why don't you go to a renewal service?" referring to the charismatic religious group my Italian teacher also attended.

We did go, and I held on to her hand, hoping at some point she'd burst out laughing and tell me we had to get out of there, and go to the beach like we'd done that time before when she explained that oral sex could be reciprocal and she talked about cosmic journeys.

That was after school one day—one of realest, most beautiful afternoons of my entire adolescent life—and she came
and got me and took me to the beach, where I confessed I
didn't know how to swim. "Oh, if I'd known, I would've
brought my niece," as if my physical inability rendered me
somehow less interesting, but the fact that she said this so
calmly, not wanting to hurt me, was a new experience: in my
family lexicon everything was meant to wound, but it turned
out you could say things for what they were, without leaving
any marks or damage. That day someone stole her car stereo,
and she didn't even blink, just said it was "negative karma."
I'd only read about women like this in books.

She loaned me the diaries of Judith Malina, rekindling my
longing to grow up in a Central European family, with books
spread everywhere on the rug. That man she loved from the
theater, she had a dream once that he cut his hair, and she
called to tell him; he laughed on the other end and said it was
a sign of great changes to come. Ever since, when people I
care about get a haircut, I'm afraid of losing them, and I observe this slight change with sorrow.

At the charismatic service I'd gone to with my teacher, we
were surrounded by timeless altar boys and special ed teachers who called out to Jesus Christ like they would their partner, but their voices were jarring, their convulsions fake. I
soon realized how much she believed in all this, that even if
she left the school at some point, she'd keep attending these
services.

She came to my home for dinner once; she'd prepared a

batch of chicken legs seasoned with cayenne, onion, and some other unidentifiable spice, a dish she learned from an old boyfriend of hers, an African (and so, her insistence that we learn the entire nomenclature of that continent: naming as an act of love), but when she looked away, we slipped our chicken to the dog. My teacher asked my mother why she never wanted to know when I'd be coming home at night or why she wasn't worried about leaving me alone. "She's free, and she better get used to it," my mother told her, not the least bit embarrassed. "She's sixteen—she can take care of herself. Like I did at her age." My teacher shook her head and gave my arm a loving squeeze. "Girls need protecting," she said. "If you're not careful, they wind up disappearing." Meanwhile, so I'd seem more normal to my friends, I sometimes pretended my mother had given me a curfew, though she hadn't.

My relationships with boys were complicated, even when I didn't want these complications. When we turned eighteen, we had parties at the civic center, and boys from other towns would often attend. At one of these parties, I took my plastic cup and went out and sat on the crumbling cement steps next to a tall, curly-haired boy in my grade, though in a different section. Maybe I liked him, but I'd only just decided that evening: he was available.

We were chatting when a drunk friend came over and dropped down beside us; these boys were in the same class. My drunk friend started talking about one of his most vivid memories from when he was young. Though he was hard to understand, we managed to figure out that one of the most traumatic episodes in *his* life was when *my* father held my brother, mother, and me hostage out on the balcony, my father with a knife to his own throat, and the whole town watching. The neighbors rushed out, women with sweaters draped over their shoulders and hands to their throats; maybe someone called the carabinieri, but they were all mummified with the passive thrill of witnessing a suicide. Their entire being pulsed with expectation; they hoped it wouldn't happen, but they couldn't wait to hear a body hit the ground.

For me, that incident was only partly true: my father stopped when he got tired, or maybe he noticed me and my brother shrugging, not really able to believe this horror, not really frightened, more on the alert, trying to defuse this. My mother was the only one who was trembling. I hadn't thought about this for years—I didn't even remember this friend in the crowd. "It was awful—I'll never forget it," he said, blond hair shaking, while all I wanted was for him to leave, and yes, I could forget it: he liked me when I was little, and I'd never liked him, and even if his infatuation had been over for some time, he couldn't seem to help himself, telling this other boy what a troubled, violent childhood I'd had, how when my father came to town, we pushed furniture up against the door and barricaded ourselves inside for days. I didn't remember a knife blade at his throat; I didn't really remember my father's sneer or his peppy, clownlike motions; I didn't remember who was down below. But I do remember sitting there on the steps outside a birthday party, with my peach-colored dress pulled over my knees and my arms crossed, beside a boy I barely knew and might have liked, trying to make light of all this, draining my cup, tearing it to pieces, with my high, broken laughter, even after that curly-haired boy got up with some fumbling excuse and went inside to get his friends and ride back with them to their town, thirty kilometers away. I see myself sitting there, staring at my legs and hands, the communal rosebushes, their petals chewed up by insects and crushed beneath my feet. The humiliation of my nice dress, my hair done in ringlets, disco music pouring from the building, and me only wanting someone to flirt with, among the statues covered in lichen where so many of us had received our first kiss. It was clear I had to leave.

There's not a single act of violence in my life that I can recall without laughing.

The Girl Absent
for Personal Reasons

I was growing up, and the word "Basilicata" never appeared on TV or in crossword puzzles. Near the end of high school, I started testing out a hysterical form of isolation, disappearing from public life, shutting myself up at home for entire days. I forced myself to be a lonely thing, as if lonely things had never existed before me.

I'd become a truculent friend, an unbearable daughter, and if I hadn't left for college, I would have officially become a tarot card, a character reduced to the literalness of her existence, just like my mother.

She was the Witch, the Madwoman, the Hermit, but these cards were out of balance, because as the town grew deserted—many of us leaving for college, never to return, the cities stealing our accents—Lovers were lost, and Popes, and Emperors, and all that was left were the Suicides and Adversaries.

Predicting the future with those cards was impossible—even my mother stopped trying: the library had flooded years earlier and no one had saved the books, allowing mold to bloom on *Fahrenheit 451* and the light of *Lolita*, fire of my loins, to fizzle out underwater. The low birth rate forced my old elementary school into mixed-level classes and taking in children from nearby towns. While there were hunters, the wild boar population was so out of control, boars would wander into the center of town at night and people carried shotguns to work. During the winter you could walk the whole length of the town, eight kilometers, from the *n' ped a terr* houses collapsed in the earthquake to the subsidized housing, and you'd never run into a single person; the wind was so strong it tore open windows.

For work, those young people still in town depended on construction, madness, and oil. Some still worked for construction companies full time; others worked for the mental rehab centers opening up in empty buildings; while the lucky few were hired as security guards for the oil wells.

At my university, I had to read John Davis' *Land and Family in Pisticci*, Banfield's amoral familism theory, and Ernesto de Martino's *Magic: A Theory from the South*, but in my view, these were outdated portrayals and didn't give a real sense of the region: true, a community might decide a citizen's destiny, from cradle to casket; true, the exchange unit wasn't money but family—and family's not something we actually had, we'd always been bad at family—but the life I led in Basilicata had been much more undisciplined, more anarchic, almost modern.

A whole lot had changed since the fifties: the rules had changed, but since they were a lot closer to those rules American teenagers followed, anthropologists found them boring: girls having an identity crisis didn't stomp on spiders in the throes of possession; they painted their nails and got drunk; boys didn't play a pipe or set fire to straw figures of Jesus Christ; in their efforts to embody a more modest god, they pulled on a Ronaldo Inter T-shirt.

Their most archaic form of entertainment was on the night of March 19, the feast of Saint Joseph, when they lit bonfires, though this happened less and less; some kids would shoot improvised horror movies with killer foxes, invent stories of black masses, but it was an esoterism already ruined by the internet.

Even when I traveled abroad, I'd hear, "Ah—Basilicata! *Christ stopped at Eboli!*," as though we still went around on the back of a mule and slipped our menstrual blood into our poor victim's coffee, to make him fall in love with us. I don't know who met the criteria for that fame, that notion of phantom civilization, but it wasn't us, even if we were surrounded by empty towns that had surrendered to landslides, and Matera, with its tuff-rock caves, was about to become a *New York Times* destination.

A few years ago, I went to see the ravines for the first time, though they were only fifteen minutes from my mother's apartment. I might see these *badlands* in a Terrence Malick movie and long to disappear into them, but it wasn't the same watching them go by, out the bus window, every morning on my way to school.

Our astronomical geography teacher—a moody, virginal string bean who sometimes just stood there, silent, for fifteen minutes straight—had tried to explain to us that we came from immortal geologies; around here you found apocalyptic and lunar landscapes, which would be an incredible tourist draw—everything else would seem trivial in comparison—but with that nasty ringworm typical of some Lucanian towns, the invasion would never come: something in the ecosystem rebelled, and denied every spore. This was true, but somehow I'd stayed and my mother had stayed: we hadn't taken root, but we hadn't been swept away, either, proof that nature's not just made up of winners and losers; the greater part of it just remains and winds up forgotten. Our teacher had explained how the ravines were formed, what karstification was, why we were especially vulnerable to landslides in this area, but I never paid attention and only thought about what he'd said on this first visit: years after leaving, I discovered I'd grown up in the desert.

When everyone disappears, a community can't rely on what it has but must create new plants to store up water, must open veins in the drought-cracked earth: lately, my mother's town has experienced some fluctuations with new oil wells and the arrival of some African refugees who, with all of Italy's bureaucratic red tape, are still stuck in a municipal building. Until recently, there was also a group home in town for recovering addicts, kids escaped from troubled families or suffering from serious psychiatric problems. It was these fluctuations that I wanted to talk about, their disruptive presence in a territory known only for hypnotic sunsets and briganti caves. I wanted to discuss this with a writer friend who had tried to get over heartbreak with a group trip to Basilicata, organized by some American artists. He'd gone to see the Aliano ravines and thought about what I'd told him about my arrival there.

"It's like a Wild West tale. No—a Fantasy West tale," he'd said as we walked by gas stations and into the lilac-gray sunset one fading London evening, in my new life.

"One day, a little girl and her family land their spaceship in a new world, and all around them, there's only dust"—he was making wide, sweeping gestures—"and then the outlaws come, and the priests . . ." I started laughing. Entertaining, yes, but it didn't play out like that. His version freed me from my humiliating childhood, but at the same time, it reduced my life to a fairy tale, a timeless story, impossible to unravel, while all I wanted was to catch that wolf I'd pretended to see in the forest, so I could slit its throat and keep on lying.

One day my girlfriends still living in town took me to see the oil-drilling facility. Actually, we only drove around it since we weren't allowed on the grounds. We climbed up a hill to take in the entire plant, and I was shocked by those three giant rigs, the same feeling I have at the sight of a wind turbine up close. A vertigo even worse than what I get from skyscrapers.

I told them what all this reminded me of and one of them said, "You say it's like going into outer space, but you know, if there's one thing we have around here, it's our feet on the ground." She was a therapist, and I'd always adored her for not tanning and for using SPF 50 sunscreen, even in winter, while I was clueless about this sense of protection; my brother and I didn't go to doctors. I was especially obsessed with these Lucanian women like me, all of them intent on slicing through cobwebs and slipping out of that marginal world, ready to forget; sylvan, solitary girls, unlikely in these parts. "Every person I know is like a landslide," she told me once while we were out walking her dog.

The rigs wouldn't draw oil directly from the ground but help raise layers of rock for further processing and extraction. There'd be no flashes of flame, no iron stakes swallowed up from pressure underground, no workers' faces encased in tar; the whole plant seemed sanitized and surgical, far more modest than the desires it unleashed. The desires: as girls, all we ever wanted was for the mystery not to unfold, and we were swelled up like leeches waiting for someone or something to blow us apart, but when I returned to my town, I found no trace of that invisible humor we once spilled, not one trace of our past explosions.

I walk up the hill to my mother's apartment, past the building where the African boys are staying, their lives run by a co-op; I'll often see them sitting out on the balcony, but I can't bring myself to say hello. I'd like to tell them that we were a threat once, that this will pass for them, too; this neglect will only be a smell, a whiff they catch, on a side street, in a new life.

As for tarot cards, my personal arcana are the Hermit and the Moon, the same Moon my mother drew when she was pregnant with me that now dominates her living room and is fading over time. On her website, an amateur fortune-teller says that for those born under these two arcana, "The essence is illumination, but the origin is darkness."

England

—◆—

The Purple Rubber Band

There is a cemetery in Calcutta for the officers of the East India Company; though cause of death is not written on any tombstones, those buried must have died from typhus or in a duel or shipwreck. The cemetery, on Park Street, is filled with Gothic, moss-softened sepulchers, stone carcasses scattered by Indo-Saracenic temples covered in a tangle of plants. And among that putrid, brackish plant growth, you'll also find Charles Dickens' son, a lieutenant, deeply in debt, who died of an aneurysm; his father had discouraged him from writing books.

When I walked through that cemetery (I was twenty at the time), I had the sensation of being in two different hemispheres at once, like a video game, with the heroine walking through two parallel worlds on the same screen: on one side was a country I'd never seen but felt tied to—England—and on the other side was India, where my blood felt thicker with each passing day. If I unraveled the mystery of one country, the other would surrender as well.

Beyond that cemetery were Victorian buildings corroded by the steamy weather, on a street of offices and British institutions with gamboge-colored ironwork and domes. The buildings felt like steampunk relics, what Western capitals might become after decades of climate change. A colonial past predicting a possible future. I wandered around Calcutta, software company employees everywhere, millions of workers in store-bought clothes parading past, pressed together, endlessly, and it was easy to imagine that British cities, overheated with ambition and overwhelmed by pollution, might look like this one day.

I wasn't expecting all the churches with blackened rooftops in Calcutta, or the invading crows pecking along the road; on my way back to the hostel, I'd cling to the redbrick walls to shelter from black clouds of birds. I'd never seen a place so Gothic, burnt-Gothic, with statues of winged women disintegrating in the sun.

At first I stayed connected, sending emails about all this to people back home. I was traveling with my friend Francesca, and after a couple of weeks, we decided to disappear. It would be one of my last trips without internet, the most spiritual decision I made back then.

Yet nothing around me, not even the lack of telecommunications, made me feel I was outside history or in some tropical,

Conrad-style nightmare, with the country's postal stations, bacterial hours, and expectations.

When we arrived, we took a taxi at the Delhi airport, a forty-minute trip to our hostel on streets I thought would be more worn, almost nonexistent, but instead had traffic lights on timers. The first smell I caught of India, much to my surprise, was disinfectant. I saw shacks crowded up against hotels with names like *Baby Las Vegas* and Christmas lights hanging off buildings and faded pink Coca-Cola signs and men practically shuffling along in the street, their shoes were so flimsy. I paused to stare at an asphyxiated girl in a petticoat and silver veil who was trying to get her electric bicycle started. Then I spotted a bunch of little boys below an underpass, piled one on top of the other, surrounded by tires. They were almost like the punks in the East Village years ago.

I'd failed to get to England on a trip that year, so Francesca suggested we go to India.

In the summer of 2005, after our college exams, I had friends over so I could empty out my freezer and get rid of my leftovers; then Francesca and the other girls and I took a walk around the dorm, feeling strangely elated. We kept repeating a terrorist's claim that the apocryphal gospels of the web had reported: "We'll turn Rome into a graveyard"; one girl had a dream about fire hydrants washing blood out of Termini station. But Rome was still there, geopolitically ignorant and ignored, and the terrorists blew up King's Cross station in London instead. We all left, quietly fretting, for break.

My boyfriend and I had planned on spending a week in England and we'd already bought our tickets and reserved our hotel, but after the bombings we changed our minds, deciding to take a bus tour through Scotland. A change of plans was normal: terrorism still had a grip on our imagination, inspiring an urge for safety that would become less and less relevant or plausible.

We enjoyed Scotland. We stayed at farms that had horses, but we kept thinking about that other city, the one we'd missed. All we saw of London was Victoria station, where we got our bus to head north, frightened and regretting our decision not to stay.

These days, a few meters from where the bombing occurred, Tracey Emin's neon phrase stands out: "I want my time with you." When I pass by it, I recall all the yearning that made me go searching for England so many years ago; I stop by some girls taking pictures of that glowing fuchsia writing, and I'm jealous at their wonder.

Mistaking a place for a love story was something I did as soon I arrived in India: I felt like I was learning about a man through his lover, their bond and mutual resentments something of a muddle for me, but I also got the distinct impression that they resembled one another, just like people do when they've been together too many years.

Our travels in India ended with a thirty-hour, no-speed train ride from Calcutta to Delhi. My friend and I were glad we could finally kick back; our compartment mates changed, we played cards, bought trinkets off peddlers. A newlywed couple came in, along with the woman's brother, a tall, very handsome boy in a turban, his face shiny with fever. He had liver disease and needed surgery, which could only be performed in Delhi. As a girl, Francesca had briefly dreamed of becoming a doctor, so she talked with the sister, trying to be helpful, telling her what she knew.

I went everywhere with a purple rubber band around my wrist, and I kept saying that if I lost it, something awful would happen. I'd been in Hindu temples and Buddhist monasteries without being so much as nicked by a religious thought; the only faith I had was in this thing I'd brought from home. I wasn't drawn to the faces of the dancers with a thousand arms behind their back; I'd learned a spiritual revolution wasn't included in the price of the trip, but I also wasn't bothered by other tourists and their expectations, by the Jewish hippies I met or the heroin addicts with their matted hair. How were Moroccan snake charmers bothering anybody? I was the one who was ridiculous, sleeping under my mosquito netting and feeling like an anthropologist, but only then, not anyplace else. Me, expecting to explore my own heart—but endless cows and red henna slashes on passing foreheads and startlingly different cities coming into view—even a vinyl-glue fog when I awoke one morning before the Himalayas. None of this carried me from the realm of observation to that of emotion. The one thought I fixed on was how class and caste fed off each other.

A few hours before our arrival on our trip from Calcutta to Delhi, I stirred to the sounds of the train and the wind and beneath these, a dim litany, a lullaby. I touched my wrist like always, but my rubber band wasn't there, so I got down from my bunk to wake Francesca, shaking her shoulders, upset, and then I realized her eyes were already open; she was staring at the family across the compartment.

The woman was rocking her brother as he lay over the seat, limp, arms hanging. He had died during the night. The conductor said they couldn't halt the train; they'd have to wait until the next stop. I wrapped a blanket around Francesca, trying not to vomit, and we rocked each other as well, trying to ward off the cold.

We were wailing, could barely breathe through our sobs; we'd never seen a dead body and with all those hours we'd spent together it felt like we knew him, though we'd only spoken through gestures. His family stared at us, dazed, not understanding all the fuss we were making, why we found this to be so important. And then, before they got off the train, they smiled at us, perhaps to make us understand that we shouldn't take life so seriously.

Then we reached Delhi and the modern middle class ashamed of rats and men in manholes, in among visiting intellectuals who would invoke the plague if it meant they could tell the story.

Without that trip to India, before even seeing it, learning of its reflection in the blueprints of another city, without witnessing the depth of its classism and its sacred indifference, I would never have understood a thing about England, no matter how many years I lived there.

In First Person

I arrived in London at age twenty-seven, on September 4, 2011, an unusual day of pouring rain. One month after the Tottenham riots, six years before the Grenfell Tower fire.

I'd come with my partner, but his company immediately sent him on to Darmstadt, to the European Space Operations Centre. Famous contemporary music courses had been taught in that town; John Cage even played there. I read this on Wikipedia, trying to make sense of our being apart. While he wrote code, I scraped mold off the walls of our newly rented house and walked in the garden; I lived for the weekends, when he came home. The rest of the time I spent barricaded inside, hands crossed over my chest, an accurate imitation of a ghost. Without my noticing, I'd become a wife.

There's a famous Unitarian church nearby with a mural

dedicated to Mary Wollstonecraft; if you look up, you'll see the inscription *The birthplace of feminism*, on a commemorative medallion. Mary Wollstonecraft moved here in 1784 to reinstate her school for girls; back then the area was full of libertarians who supported the American Revolution and women's rights. Oliver Cromwell and Daniel Defoe would pass through, and for a time, Edgar Allan Poe lived somewhere in the area. Not far from here is the Mildmay Club, one of the last working men's clubs in London, where a beer costs three pounds, but the members are dying off or moving away; on weekends, they rent the club out for weddings or as a movie soundstage.

After moving to Newington Green, Wollstonecraft wrote *A Vindication of the Rights of Woman*, the reason the Unitarian Church is considered the birthplace of feminism. Though this doesn't change the fact that I moved here for love, and I wasn't doing anything with my life. Her daughter, Mary Shelley, also fell in love when she was young, like I did, but she wrote a brilliant book and invented science fiction.

Another woman deciding the destiny of this neighborhood where I live: in the sixteenth century, one of the area's inhabitants, Henry Percy, became secretly engaged (without permission) to the future mistress, then wife of Henry VIII. Percy tried to announce that they'd already slept together and that it would weigh on him if he didn't marry her, but due to the girl's lower social status, the marriage was prevented anyway. Around ten years later, Percy was forced to testify during Anne Boleyn's trial for adultery and he collapsed and was carried out after hearing she'd been sentenced to death.

The street I see every morning when I step out the door is named for Anne Boleyn; I'm caught between a suffragette and a queen who lost her head.

The places I fell in love with first in London: a cemetery, a movie theater, and a skate park. The Abney Park cemetery is one of the seven great private cemeteries in the city, but it's more rundown than that Park Street cemetery in Calcutta; and here you'll find the graves of all the radical nonconformists who passed this way. The Rio Cinema is over a hundred years old, and its founder was the entrepreneur Clara Ludski, who decided to convert her auctioneer's shop to a movie picture house, full of statues and domed ceilings. When I started going, it was still famous for showing movies even at two in the morning, old horror pictures normally, or cult movies from the eighties and nineties, an after-hours sanctuary for street people; there wasn't a merchandise corner yet in the lobby, no T-shirts for sale with a Rio Cinema logo.

The Stockwell Skatepark is south of here, on the other side of the river, less than a kilometer from Brixton. In 2011 it didn't have a Wikipedia page or a history, for me. Now I know it's called Brixton Beach and was funded by the city in 1978. And a nearby store sells skateboards, but there wasn't one before. With no signs up, the park looked like something that just happened to be there, almost completely surrounded by squat, brown council houses on the verge of being knocked down to make way for new construction. I liked going, with

all the people leaning over their balconies watching those
kids performing stunts on skateboards and BMXes from
close up.

It was the only place where I could feel calm. I'd go on
afternoons and sit and watch the boys and girls sailing down
the cement bank. I'd shut my eyes and hear the wheels swish-
ing, the sliced air, the stuck landing, back in my freelance
days of no friends and nothing to do. I'd watch those teenagers and not participate myself, like when I was a child, sitting
by my brother, watching him play *Vampire* or *Max Payne*: I
found this comforting, someone else to keep the story going
without me having to take any responsibility for it myself.
I'm a good navigator; sometimes, to make me feel useful, my
brother told me to check the maps and instructions, although
he didn't need me to, but when I have to decide on my own,
when I have to blast away in first person with my machine
gun, I die at once—I don't know how to fight my way out.
Those were the closest moments I had with my brother, when
I hoped his fictional character wouldn't get wounded. I never
grabbed the controller, was never that girl who wanted to
take over. It was enough for me to help develop the story, to
root for him not to die on the screen, and I did the same with
the kids at the skate park, waiting for them to make their
heroic leaps and draw their perfect perimeters.

I emigrated from Italy during a strange period in history.
During Arab Spring, the Tottenham riots when Mark Dug-
gan was killed by the police, the war in Syria, the Occupy
movement, and Berlusconi's fall through a European ruling;

everywhere I went, I sensed rage and longing. An obsessive, hammering sense of change, partly news-fed, partly self-induced, a fever each of us would describe differently that was destined to waste away, into countless personal stories. For me, the year 2011 was the only break I had from feeling nostalgic; life now doesn't seem to reflect that historical juncture, a collective error we haven't resolved. There was a brief window when we might have laid claim to the present, but we didn't. And now, years later, time has collapsed and shattered yet again, and we still haven't staked our claim. Ten years ago, I walked by the occupiers' tents at St. Paul's Cathedral, I flipped through books at the local library, so much Stephen King (he might have taught us a thing or two about slipping into that parallel present, about inverting the laws of time), and I got the distinct feeling that something was collapsing.

It was great not feeling nostalgic—though I'd moved for this, choosing London the way a teenager would, with a romanticized notion of punk and the daily urban apocalypse. I wasn't remotely afraid of the darkness that years later would make me lie in bed for hours on end, watching the foxes scuffle in the garden.

I did meet at least one real punk: my landlady is one of the last of the seventies women. She doesn't live in London anymore—she retired to the country, like most of her generation.

The first time I saw her, she just showed up at our door with her white hair down to her waist and her witchy, pointy-toed booties; Tom Waits called those shoes "cockroach impalers." She showed us around, then took us over to a friend's to sign the lease, which by law required a witness.

The "witness" was one of the founding members of the Swell Maps, an experimental British band and precursor to post-punk. I stood ramrod straight in his living room piled high with dusty cassette tapes and cylinders and skulls, and I babbled on about writing for an independent music magazine, while he sneered at me, like I'd made it all up on the spot. His garden was stuffed full of shopping carts and things he'd recycled, chipped teacups God knows how old, and when we left, the sun milky and corrosive in a postnuclear sky, I took my boyfriend's hand and thought my adult life had finally begun. At the same time, I was afraid that nothing so beautiful as that afternoon would ever happen to me again: this wasn't just something I'd read about in my counterculture books—I'd actually seen these people, spoken to them.

My landlady is a visual artist, and she left all her handmade furniture and items in the house for us. I was deciding what to keep and picked up a black-and-white photo of a wrapped-up mummy; she asked if I wanted it, but it was too grim for me. "A friend's self-portrait—he just killed himself." She giggled, then said, "Oh well, we can always chuck it," and I followed her from room to room then, hoping she'd tell me the story of everything I saw. An ex of hers built the bed I'd sleep in, a gilded four-poster she had considered setting on fire to celebrate the end of their relationship. But they'd stayed friends. She always stayed friends. She hadn't gotten rid of a single phone number of all the men she'd met. When something broke in the house, she never sent over a repairman or plumber; one of her old lovers showed up. I've spent years preparing cups of tea for men who are all alike and have come to fix our damage: they all have a band and a divorce in their past. My landlady is what my friend Sara and I define as the quintessential cat lady: a woman who's had many men pursue her but only ever really loved one, and after that, never opened her heart to a man again. She only has sexual relations, which end in mutual esteem; she receives her ex-boyfriends at lunchtime and makes them coffee and listens to their heartfelt anguish, then dismisses them with a bit of no-nonsense wisdom and goes back to feeding the cats. She's our hero, this cat lady; sometimes we kill off her true love in a motorcycle accident.

The only Englishmen she's truly fond of belong to a generation much different from my own. The latest, Bond, told me that before he dies he wants to see the British cemeteries in India, all the young officers and colonels buried there, and then he wants to buy a boat to help migrants reach Greece. He told me this while he was breaking up bathroom tiles without wearing a mask, mouth open, smiling, flashing those teeth that only certain people have, my mother's teeth, that at some point, even with money, are beyond repair. He was oozing a hodgepodge of imperialism and romanticism over the Mediterranean, so typical of left-leaning Brits. I asked him to tell me about his trips to California to see the Dead

Kennedys; I wanted to hear what moshing in the pit was like back then, but I came to realize that no matter how fascinating I found his stories, they didn't belong to me. This was their history, not mine.

I'd moved to London for the wrong reasons, and I had to learn how to live there.

There, Where the Shadows Lie

My favorite word in English is *marshes*. It's the plural of the noun *marsh*: acquitrino in Italian. It comes from the Old English *mersc*, and the Proto-Germanic *mori*, "body of water." Other favorite words resemble these, all of them describing a landscape. *Moor* from the Old English *mor*: brughiera in Italian. *Morass*: palude. Each of them owing something to the Proto-Indo-European root *mer*. *Mer*, meaning "to hurt," "to die," or even "sea."

Mor also reminds me of Mordor, the dark, evil wasteland in *The Lord of the Rings*. In high school, when I read J. R. R. Tolkien's saga for the first time, a classmate texted me that I was "headed to Mordor by way of a swamp." At the time I didn't fully understand what he meant, but it's an opinion

I've grown accustomed to in London: those living in the city always feel the influence of a dark, distant tower, an unease carried in the air, spreading from an unknown source, perhaps hidden in the skyscrapers, in the channels of the River Lea, which, some days, made you feel possessed, burdened by a crushing, grounding weight, reverberating in your bones even while you couldn't name it, something that for some becomes the glowing emanation of despair, turning them to sentinels to push aside, to avoid becoming like them, on some lo-fi adventure trip.

I walk around London without going through iron gates or by volcanoes or thorny moors, I keep going, on asphalt muddied by rain, feeling a joy and daring that eventually turn to weariness, but I keep going, and catching sight of the tower in the distance, I can't resist—like every slash of dusty, purple light that takes me by surprise, of those sunsets, rarely seen, descending over the buildings—I'm held, possessed, by the force of the tower, by the light of the tower.

A city founded on water, London also takes over the house, in the form of moisture and spores, sending translucent cobwebs over the walls that resurface with every passing season. I only forget about this once I'm outside and stop smelling that odor of the forest, the fecund house, something I can't control no matter how hard I try. It doesn't matter how many chemicals I try, how many home remedies like dishtowels soaked in vinegar and lemon juice: that smell of putrid water remains.

I head to Clissold Park and take its *desire paths*, eroded, shaped through all the humans and animals that have walked them. A worn path from one place to another. In Italian, this would be a "scorciatoia," a shortcut, and the first time I came across the expression, *desire path*, I lingered over the word "desire," which confused me, tricked me: I was convinced that *desire paths* were made up, what people imagined as they walked through the city at all hours, the places they liked to get lost in, or slip into, lit spots on a private map.

These days, it's almost impossible to get lost in London, and not just because there's a GPS on every cell phone: every interstitial space in the city, anywhere you might cross into a new district, has a map on the corner. And there's always a dot showing "You are here." These directions might keep you from getting lost, but they also make you feel exposed and concerned that you might be seen, what Virginia Woolf experienced on certain days, what Jean Rhys and Sylvia Plath felt, too: a city anxiety. Whatever happened to that stunned feeling, of knowing absolutely nothing about a city and fooling yourself into thinking that everything you discover is being discovered for the first time? What space is left for desire when everything is so transparent?

Years ago, I answered a want ad I found on a website. A position I thought I might be qualified for: an art curator who worked with the major presses doing photography books was looking for an assistant to catalog his archives and help with purchases. I went to Clapham and rang the bell to an enormous Tudor-style brick house, and was welcomed by an affable, middle-aged British gentleman. His living room was filled with rugs, books and records everywhere; on the brief trip to his study, I noticed a biography on the Smiths and DVD cases for TV series I'd also watched. A good sign, I thought. During our chat, he asked me to talk about myself and my tastes, then he insisted on showing me his manuscript about our favorite Italian writer: he couldn't believe I loved Cesare Pavese, too, and I couldn't believe he'd written about him. At one point he proclaimed, "I felt closer to John Peel than my own father," and a shockwave ran through me: while music was very important to me—I wrote about it all the time back then—I'd never say a DJ was closer to me than someone I knew. This kind of disregard, so elegant and controlled, was startling. Some British people were so indifferent to conventions, to family; I had the sneaking suspicion I'd alienated them with my infrastructure of nerves and feelings, my desire, my yearning to connect, like a creeping vine. Not this man though: I could tell he liked me and that he'd take me on for a trial run, but he still had one last question for me. How did I feel about working with him in the room while he was naked? He'd quit his job at the publishing house for this very reason: he and his wife were naturists, as was his son, and all their friends. Over the summer, they all shared a villa together in the Pyrenees—I could come, too, if I liked—and they held symposiums while wandering around without any clothes on. It was a lifestyle that finally brought him a sense of inner peace; even the girl I might replace became a nudist in the end. I tried to assume an appropriate expression, but he saw right through me, could tell how uncomfortable I felt, how out of place. I hadn't said anything—I wasn't sure I could face a trial period—and he shook my hand and said he'd think about it and let me know. He phoned the next day and told me he was sorry because he really liked me, but he'd found another girl who didn't have issues with him or his family being naked.

When I told my mother about this, she pulled out all her obsolete hippie principles, that I was such a prude, that she couldn't believe I was her daughter—what's wrong with being naked and totally comfortable with yourself? Other people thought it was creepy, some kind of sex-for-hire thing, but that's not the impression I got, not at all: he seemed almost monastic, as though he clung to the idea of staying undressed, convinced this was the true antidote to the sadness I could sense in almost everything he said.

I wasn't a prude, but I was confused by the sex I noticed in London, in the metro, in bars, at street parties: it was anything but carnal; I'd go to clubs, and teenagers would be everywhere, oozing a negative, android energy. I had a hard time finding people who didn't seem disgusted by kissing. Yet they were constantly touching—maybe I was the only one who didn't perceive a sense of real desire in any of this.

Literature haunts the streets where I live. Around ten years ago, there was a gang around here, they called themselves Soldiers of Shakespeare, but they never had much of a fortune. The name paid homage to Shakespeare Walk, a residential street in the area. Going by one day, I saw a young couple: he had two cans of beer in plastic bags, she was in a wheelchair a few meters away. They were screaming at each other, the boy saying he couldn't take it anymore, he was going to lose it. Then she started sobbing and shouted: "You'd fuck me? You'd fuck me even in this chair?" He threw his bags down, knelt in front of her, and started kissing and licking her knees below her shorts, saying he'd fuck her, he loved her. I went by trying to be as discreet as possible, resisting the urge to turn around. They seemed very much in love, very attracted to each other, an avalanche of desire. A spark in the darkness, so glaring and so rare, that if I turned back to see, they might flutter out of existence.

Office Clothes

In cafés, in shopping centers, in shared offices, I was incredibly shy; I only truly felt comfortable at the hair salon, and I made friends with the Romanian stylists I saw every three months. They'd tell me about their Tinder dates—the worst took them to smoke pot in the multiplex parking lot, the girls in their sequin dresses bought online—and they'd update me with photos of their weddings and the bathroom they were putting in back home, in Eastern Europe. After Brexit, a haircut became an excuse: now I go to fume with someone else who gets it, as if beauty salons were the meeting places of the new secret Carbonari society. For a time, these girls were my only friends, even if I didn't have their phone numbers. The only ones around that I thought of as close. Every time I walked in, they asked me how my mother

was, if I was thinking of getting married, and they wanted
to discuss Venice, though they knew a lot more about Venice
than I ever did. I felt strangely euphoric around them, the
same way I felt with my female colleagues at the translation
agency where I worked for a while; the offices were located
in a basement in Islington, a sweatshop for the creative class,
with poor lighting and bad ventilation, outside all work health
regulations, a security camera monitoring all the sneaking out
past the fire door for a cigarette; once a week we'd go have
french fries near the gas station and talk about arranging a
marriage to get our permanent residency, like we were the
updated version of one of those romantic comedies from the
eighties about marrying for a green card.

At the height of the Vietnam War, a generation of Americans responded to the massacre of their peers with the psychedelic movement, the New Age movement. When veterans
returned from the Middle East after the wars in the early
2000s, PTSD contributed to the spreading practice of mind-
fulness, fortune-telling, yoga, in a new landscape of perva-
sive salvation. The 2008 financial crisis did quite a bit for the
field of personal well-being: in London, there are sanctuaries
that nurture the peaceful retreat into oneself (mantras re-
cited, people crouching like spiders to wash off the day's
impurities), sanctuaries that colonize every quarter, ignoring
the basic mechanics of competition—you can't go thirty meters without running into another spiritual-wellness center.
They have display windows devoted to the sun, to the moon,
to crystals; the word "cleansing" is everywhere, and here I

was growing up thinking this had something to do with ethnic purity. I seem to wind up in these classes sometimes, and I'll catch sight of others in their supple poses and can feel their disapproval over mine, so inflexible, so uncleansing.

At this point, there's nothing in my neighborhood or the surrounding areas that's unfamiliar to me, but I still feel as insecure as the day I arrived. Every time I walk someplace different, or I wind up in the labyrinth of streets beyond the river, I have that feeling of being the new girl at school; I'm terrified that my clothes will be wrong, that my "social language" will be embarrassing, that I won't have the basic rules down for the right laugh when the most popular boy in school cracks a joke. I'm terrified they'll make fun of my accent, tell me, "I was here first." For me, wandering from one point to another in a modern city means searching for a relatively comfortable, anonymous spot to stop just the right amount of time to bring out that new girl and make her feel awkward.

I've reached the point of feeling ashamed to say where I live, because it's almost like I'm claiming to be an authority on this place, when I'm not; the longer I live in London, the more my impostor syndrome climbs. I still haven't learned how to live in a new city; I still don't know how to pass through it without turning everything into a testament or heartbreak.

Living in East London is like getting a part in a forty-year-old sci-fi movie where the future is now. Minus the flying cars and holograms already in the comic books of the era. I stroll around, replicants of me everywhere, all of us in our bright blue steelworker jackets, walking by fake souks with Turkish and Caribbean signs announcing, "Everything for ninety-nine cents!" and "Best jerk chicken in town," and they're all a part of the youth-entertainment industry, while pretending to be Turkish baths or pool halls, though owned by *Vice* or some other magazine.

A few months ago, I'd just left the supermarket when I was stopped by a woman around fifty, in a regulation office uniform: slightly flared black pants, leather ballet flats, white blouse. She asked me for a pound, and I told her I didn't have any cash. I was about to leave, but then I whipped around and asked if an Oyster card would help her get back to her flat. I figured someone must have taken her wallet. But that pound was to help her get a bed at the King's Cross hostel; she normally stayed at the large shelter past the station, but you had to reserve your bed every morning, with your best chance if you got up by six. That morning she couldn't do it, she was too tired, had some hard shifts at work. She could reserve a spot at another place for a few pounds, this one also behind the station—all she needed was one more pound. She'd learned that dressing this way got her money faster, but she did feel somewhat guilty about the kid she saw begging in front of the supermarket. Many others in the hostel did this: "They'll go buy office clothes at Primark and wear them while they're out asking for money. They pretend they're gainfully employed and lost their wallet, and that's how they manage to get by every day."

When I first arrived in London, I'd go to parties and dance with the people around me dressed like they were right out of the Polish Resistance; these days, the streets around King's Cross are filled with homeless people pretending to be in the middle class, for coins. "We're all middle class now," said Tony Blair, but he got it wrong: we're all a class disguised as another—the distribution of poverty and wealth remains the same.

It's hard to walk through East London without thinking about buying something, some transaction at an off-license, a nail bar, a vape shop. It's only when I'm roaming around the old docks and going by the old warehouses of the shipping companies that I remember what happened: this is where the addiction arrived. This is where they docked, the ships filled with spices and beasts from distant lands, where the contagious desire for new things turned to magical possession.

I don't remember what I imagined about the advancement of technology when I was a child. I know that in my late teens, with the arrival of the internet, it didn't feel like the future; the internet quickly grew trivial, as did everything that came with it. Perhaps, in childhood, the future always coincided with wonder, and as such, had to be impossible: it didn't necessarily have to foster improvement; it just had to remain a threshold I couldn't cross. The future was everything that came before a departure.

Every Person I Know Is

London has lost the night; clubs keep closing earlier and earlier.

Years ago, night buses were full of shy, frail, revolting people. They were all exquisite monsters, cheeks caved in, open-mouth kissing, turn-of-the-century cold.

Momentary happiness found in basements, when I'd go dancing underground and spend three or four hours not talking to anyone, protected by that shell I'd always envied with those bony, romantic figures I'd read about in *Please Kill Me*. When Ed Sanders said: "There's something individually apocalyptic in it—a personal apocalypse, a hardening off." For a few hours in those Kingsland basements, when I was still a girl who'd just arrived, I became an inviolable chrysalis, too, but then many of those clubs shut down, and with the eviction notices also went a layer of skin, the last veil of adolescence.

I was headed to a rave at a club called Printworks, and I stopped along the way to eat in a shopping center popular with families in Surrey Quays. I was just about to throw away my trash when a guy working there came up to me and said he'd do it, that he'd just been hired. He shook my hand and said he was from a Calabrian village, and his girlfriend managed a sports shop right next door. He introduced himself with both his first and last name. I felt slightly embarrassed: What should I do, look him up on Facebook, friend him, pass on all my accumulated wisdom and confusion from my time in London? I was smiling at him when I left, but I didn't give him my name, and I only thought about this later, on my return trip on the Overground, when the father of one of my high school classmates popped into my head. As a boy, he'd gone to work in Germany; his name was Mauro. One day on the street he heard the word *maurer*—in German, *maurer* means "mason"—and he turned around, overjoyed, certain someone was calling his name. He told this story to his daughters, explaining how alone he felt back then, to the point of hearing things, but as my friend insisted, he was also laughing at himself.

A short time later, on a Ryanair flight from Rome to London, I was sitting next to a deaf couple with two small children. They were asking me about what they should do once we landed at Stansted Airport, how to take public transportation to the city, and I said I could help. I could wait for them at passport control; I promised this, in my half-hearing, half-mute pidgin that I used with my parents. When the immigration agent let me through, I turned around to see how far along they were, and then I sped up and left, only to feel sick to my stomach on the bus.

It's like I've forgotten how to be around other people. Rather than stopping to help someone out who might be in trouble, I just wonder how much rent my acquaintances pay or what sort of job they have that they can stay here, a stubborn resistance that blots me out, turns me into someone different, a person whose voice, mannerisms, clothing choices I can't bear.

I walk quickly to shake off the androgynous ninjas, all the health fanatics kinetically crowding the streets. Everyone out there is dressed in guerrilla sportswear, in bodysuits and running shoes, as though preparing to jump into the void. They've taken over the night, with their athletic, iodate optimism, and all the ugly, monstrous people have begun to disappear or to live en masse in the station. Empathy is something I've unlearned, and now I have my citizenship in high-speed indifference.

Like a Landslide

My mother and uncles, like many people their age, have an ugly scar on their arm from their smallpox vaccination. At a family reunion, they told me they were certain they got this vaccine so they could come live in America, and they'd always considered it a "marchio dell'immigrato"—an immigration stamp—that distinguished them from others.

Obviously, the scar has nothing to do with all of that—it's just a fantasy they've cultivated over time. I'll look at myself in the mirror now and then, touch my arm, and this psychosomatic scar still doesn't show. Though I have no obvious proof, the border officers detain me at the window and subject me to longer and longer questions to the point that I feel like a spy, and this cosmopolitan life that's always seemed adventurous now just feels complicated.

I didn't inherit a single political thought from my family; what I inherited instead was a jumble of aspirations, self-pity, kabbalah, sloth, and rage that can assume the ideological orientation that's most convenient and readily available. A sad, useless genetic dowry that helped me predict Brexit and the election of Donald Trump—like I come equipped with sensors that allow me to anticipate collective agitation, though I'm far less informed than others I know who are politically active. I have a reluctant talent for recognizing disaster.

These sensors, though, don't tell me what term I should apply to this migration I'm now a part of.

When we die, maybe on our tombstone they'll write a loved one's name, what profession we had, a line from a favorite book.

What won't be written on our tombstones is our distance from home.

We're not teenagers who left in search of frontier gold, and even if we grow sick with loneliness, as happened to Old West pioneers, no one's going to point out the distance we came. No one's going to point out that my friends and I moved to England and died two thousand kilometers from where we grew up, and why might that be? Perhaps because we weren't driven by pioneer winds, didn't conquer any wastelands, didn't conjure up wells for drinking water; because we settled down in already overcrowded cities and worked near the dwellings where we slept in the humidity and incomprehension of the owners, these western outposts marked on a map in search of our kind, where not one consulate or post office, on a sort of death watch, ever noticed the distance we came; because, for many of us, our leaving wasn't really necessary or all that hard.

After Brexit, expats became immigrants like all the rest; some consider themselves stateless, others, exiles. To feel more elegant, we define ourselves as strangers.

And then there are the others, the potential migrants. What should they be called, the ones who've never left but feel someplace other than where their daily circumstances put them? The lexicon of migrations is made up of words referring to victory or failure. There are always heroics to celebrate, or deaths to mourn, but this lexicon should also include those who have never had access to leaving, who live in a distant country with only their desire or illusion; who memorize the map of another continent as though it were an oil painting they could paint themselves into, blurred into the canvas, their body, a new landscape coming into view.

In the late 1930s, the Polish writer Maria Kuncewiczowa wrote a book titled *Cudzoziemka*, which was published in Italy in 1940 with the title *La straniera*. In England it came out in 1944 under the title *The Stranger*, without the nod to the female gender. It's the reason the British edition of Albert Camus' *L'Étranger* is sometimes still called *The Outsider*. Some editors actually preferred this title, with its connotation of political exile.

Kuncewiczowa's book tells the story of Rose, a woman who feels she is a Russian exile in Poland and a Polish exile in Europe during the period between the World Wars, and she's unhappy with both. She takes out her political and romantic frustrations on her family, until she dies, her head sunken into a pillow, "hiding from the difficult world." Her story is much different from Meursault's, but both characters live in a state of refusal that renders them invincible, plus they're not exactly on their own.

Camus' stranger has an entire philosophical movement behind him: Meursault was never alone on that beach where he shot an Arab; there were rebelling ghosts to keep him company. Maria Kuncewiczowa's stranger is detestable but regal, always very lofty in her frustrations.

The European immigrants of the twentieth century took refuge in books; their condition was one that was troubled, noble, and most of all, shared, a condition determined less by individual choice than by war. There are many heirs to these strangers, including me, but since we're not in exile and have no common cause that defines our leaving, any word that does define our condition proves to be offensive—the cosmopolitanism of our privilege, an outrage—because it concerns a migration we're almost always free to choose, a migration that never founders.

Yet even here there's shame, and a sense of barely being, barely belonging.

The Exact Replica

My grandmother immigrated to Brooklyn in the sixties and adapted better than I did to London in the early 2010s, and she didn't even speak English.

I spent years feeling ashamed by this, and jealous at how quickly she had settled in.

I was born in the mid-eighties, raised at the end of modernity, art, the great novel, my life already posthumous, already defined by a series of prefixes. Maybe my grandmother read about the end-times in the Bible or was frightened when her neighbors showed her their bomb shelters, but the apocalypse wasn't an ad campaign for her generation, and disaster movies only burst on the scene when I was a child.

I grew up, like many my age, with the myth of the late

seventies in New York. Repeated destruction fantasies: all the heroin deaths in Alphabet City, the most dangerous enclave in the world; the Bronx fires. I made my pilgrimages to the Chelsea Hotel, to the room where Sid Vicious might have killed "Nauseating" Nancy, and I fell in love, at least once, with Johnny Thunders' rotten, green smile. But all the passionate yearning I ever had for a destroyed city disappeared in the summer of 2017, when the Grenfell Tower went up in flames and there was a terrorist attack on the London Bridge. After yet another sleepless night with helicopters flying overhead and then a new alarm going off, a crazed truck plowing over the sidewalk, I woke up thinking that the only thing missing now was an epidemic of hard drugs, to complete this as the exact replica of a 1970s New York: the recession, the procession from the food bank to the personal-loan bank, the austerity march for one-fifth of the population.

I have a feeling that in years to come, when I'm not living here anymore and the post-Brexit period is reassessed for its social costs, I won't be tempted to monumentalize everything that's going on at the moment. I won't talk about the great art and great music of the time; I'll talk about the Ministry of Loneliness and the Ministry of Suicide, these government agencies aimed at their prevention, because these are the things I already remember, in a present that every day is made posthumous, with some article on Brexit that I've already forgotten.

We can fail at love, at our relationship with our mother.

But when a city rejects us, when we can't seem to enter into its deepest workings, are always stuck on the other side of the glass, the denied sense of our own worth takes over, and turns to malaise. *Stranger* is a beautiful word, if you're not forced to be one. The rest of the time, it's just a synonym for mutilation, a gun we point at ourselves, and fire.

HEALTH

Mutilation was a language.
And vice versa.

—LORRIE MOORE

The Infinite Room

Every year, in February, my mother insisted we watch the Sanremo Music Festival.

For five days, we'd sit on the couch in front of the TV and listen to those uninspired songs, stunned by a deluge of roses and teased hair.

Well, at least my brother and I listened—she couldn't— she read the subtitles to follow the songs.

The melodic pop singers on that stage always put on operatic airs, waving their arms around, but with nearly all of them doing it, my mother couldn't tell any difference between their songs. She couldn't see from their stance if the song was sad or about love or social commitment; she had to trust those terse, often out-of-sync subtitles popping up.

My mother has always loved music. She grew up in a

family that was always playing music on tapes and the accordion, and enjoyed watching Neapolitan musicals, with their cloying choruses and repetitive rhythms, usually about some unexpected betrayal or a time when someone was unjustly imprisoned.

When I decided to major in anthropology in college, it felt like I was enrolling in an anti-stereotype program. I couldn't wait to learn about class, gender, and ethnicity, to see them blown apart, and discover a new kind of hybrid humanity, so I could forget all those things that had conditioned me and made me who I was. Early on, one professor told us: "By the time you're through here, you'll realize there's something to the fact that Germans are rigid. That Neapolitans steal. That Romans are bad drivers." He was being honest with us, and in some sophisticated ways, he was right. Soon we'd be reading Michael Herzfeld's *Cultural Intimacy: Social Poetics in the Nation-State*, and we made our peace.

And this is why I don't feel guilty about stereotyping my Italian American family through passionate criminal references, the great fantasies they aspired to. These were their favorite movies, their favorite songs.

Back then, I didn't know what metaphors and allegories were, and neither did my mother—when I translated a song for her, the texts of Nino D'Angelo or Mario Merola, so she could feel closer to her father, who loved those Neapolitan singers, everything seemed literal to us: the people they sang of were truly prepared to kill or die for unrequited love. Those songs were declarations of war, not transfigurations of sorrow; they were transformative acts, not passive comforts.

My mother and I were out of context.

My mother and I preferred our texts real, but we were surrounded by fiction. Fiction in the blood: delusion was common in her family—she may have been deaf, but every year, her brother Arthur still gave her a Walkman as a gift.

She'd hook one of Sony's first yellow Walkmans onto the belt loop of her jeans while she cleaned the house, and she swore she could feel the beat. "Aren't you crazy about this band?" she'd ask a guest, and this friend would turn to me with a questioning look, given the fact that my mother couldn't hear. It would be like saying he had a favorite letter in braille. Maybe, but since he wasn't blind, it wasn't the same.

To her family, my mother was, above everything else, a foreigner, an incomprehensible girl: now they live far apart, and she goes to visit her brothers every year or two, but they still don't know how to deal with the fact that she can't hear. They'll speak together and it won't be in sign language or in an immigrants' language, either: none of them know English like they should, and no one mentions disability. What's disability anyway in a household where no one speaks like anyone else?

"What's the music like?" my mother would ask when I was little and swaying to the sound of the tarantella, down in her father's basement. He'd invite her to dance, stamp his leather shoes on the floor, hoping the vibrations would sail up her calves, ripple in her hips, crash against her ribs, while his old

friends played their accordions and drank like fish, and sometimes she danced, and sometimes not. Then, there came a
point when she retreated. She stopped asking about the music,
grew increasingly weary of that game. And no matter how
much I liked to see her dance, it also made me angry, I was
annoyed by her performance, her desire to join in: her steps
were never quick enough, never in rhythm. Just like I re-
sented her laughter when we watched a movie together—if
she noticed I was laughing, she'd laugh, too, but a few seconds too late. A physical reaction, almost involuntary, whether
or not she'd understood, and in those few seconds, everything
in me turned sour.

My mother watched the Sanremo Festival like it was a
competition for the best story of the year. The texts were all
that mattered, prose poems overindulging in love and pain.

She liked singer-songwriters and had a collection of books
on music: the history of reggae, an anthology of songs from
prison, communist anthems, Patti Smith's early poems, Bob
Dylan's collected lyrics. Like her, I never wondered what those
songs sounded like when I borrowed those books; we were
both there for the story. Before someone took me to a record
shop, I didn't know Patti Smith and Bob Dylan even had a
voice. I'd experienced those musicians just like my mother—
in silence. I'd tried to imagine how they sounded, and I found
their pulse, their rhythm, the same way I did with any other
fiction writer or poet I read. And when I first heard their
voices, I wasn't disappointed, not really, but I did lose something in the bargain—a closeness to my mother. I stepped

over the line and into another world, where songs could be heard and repeated ad nauseam. In that moment, I also lost my appropriation fantasy that comes so easily when I read literature: I could no longer fill in the cracks between the words with a music that was mine alone. That's why I haven't understood the debates about Bob Dylan's Nobel Prize: to me he's always been more alive in his writing than in his voice.

The songs presented at Sanremo were less ambitious than the ones described in those books. They weren't revolutionary or inventive or prophetic, and they did nothing for the genre: the main concern of those musicians was avoiding losing someone they loved, or else losing someone they loved so they could write a song about it.

But there were exceptions. My mother and I lived for the exceptions.

In 1993, a kid named Nek got on stage to sing "In te," his song about abortion. It was emphatically pro-life, but at least it was different. In 1996, Federico Salvatore dealt with homosexuality in "Sulla porta," a song focusing on a mother rejecting her gay son. In 1999, the singer-songwriter Daniele Silvestri sang "Aria," a story ripped from the headlines about a man sentenced to die at Asinara prison.

These songs, by the way, were my first real exposure to these national, sociopolitical debates. I lived in a society where suffering didn't exist unless it could be measured by someone's physical distance from a doctor or a priest.

My mother couldn't stand fiction, so she always rooted for the songs with social repercussions, and these usually won, since they wound up discussed in the papers. I think it was her way of standing up for the victory of meaning over sound, and getting her revenge on those few mainly instrumental pieces that left people like her without a clue. So maybe it's more accurate to say that in this particular contest, my mother was searching for the best nonfiction story of the year.

Her comments about these songs: "His girlfriend really did have an abortion and now he's suffering." "How awful it must feel to be rejected by your mother." "I wonder if I could write him in prison."

My father couldn't stand fiction either. For him movies like *Scarface* and *Evil Dead* are documentaries, real-life stories. Every time I tried to explain that "this never happened," to introduce him to the subtleties of fiction, he'd protest and wave me off, sometimes enraged. If I told my mother that the movie she just saw wasn't a biopic, then that movie wasn't worth a damn. She still thinks *The Exorcist* is a realist masterpiece.

Both my parents interpret life as fact and cling to words for what they are, but they're also suspicious, like many deaf people, always afraid there are those conspiring about meanings behind their back; for my parents, a rose is truly a rose is a rose, but is it truly?

My life as a writer depends on irony and metaphor, and my parents are horrified and alienated by both. When we're together, we enter a strange territory, a language black market: I force allegories onto them, and they fight back that words are unequivocal, can't possibly have multiple meanings.

My father kept having terrible dreams after the divorce, so one year for Christmas I gave him a small white eraser. I wrote on it, "To erase bad memories," which he didn't take very well. I was just trying to be his daughter, to identify with the healing properties of objects, the literalness of things, but this wasn't my battle; it was his.

I've always thought deafness was an obstacle to their fully recognizing figurative language. As a girl, without reflecting on it, I believed a gap existed in my parents' knowledge and that I could work my hardest to fill this gap, by interpreting and swapping out words for them. According to some studies, though, there are no real differences between deaf and hearing teenagers when it comes to understanding a metaphor they might find in a novel. Irony is a bit different: apparently, deaf teenagers understand irony more as they develop, as they grow increasingly aware of a tone that inflects (or infects) the people around them. But irony is a figure of speech that arrives with a loss of innocence for all, hearing or otherwise. (The first time my mother understood an ironic joke she was fifty-five, and my brother and I just stared at her, amazed and incredibly grateful.)

For a deaf reader, the journey inside a metaphor can be slower, more winding and unpredictable, but this is true for many of us: while we rely on a shared archive of symbols when we read a work of art, our internal translations of those symbols vary. When it comes to tests for measuring reading comprehension, I do think it's a mistake if a child misses all the symbolism in *The Wonderful Wizard of Oz*, but I like that kind of mistake. If a metaphor is an accident, a revelation, a car accident, I'm always left picking up the same shattered bits of glass. I never capture, never obtain even one new splinter; I just stick to my part in the constant recycling of beauty.

I don't know if my parents were proud of not following proper grammar rules or were just too lazy to develop their skills in literacy or simply put too much trust in their senses and preferred demystifying a code that didn't pertain to them anyway, but I often think of them when I'm translating novels from one language to another: I'm no longer worried that I'm drawn to errors, that I have a soft spot for them.

Not too long ago, I found myself thinking about James M. Barrie's Neverland in *Peter Pan*. In Italian, *Neverland* has been translated as "L'isola che non c'è," The island that's not there, but honestly a literal translation of the English would be better: while "L'isola che non c'è" suggests a territory that's impossible to find or even nonexistent, the literal "Maiterra" is a refusal, the longing to cut all ties to the traditional world, and is closer to the Lost Boys' intentions. No, as a children's resounding battle cry, "Terramai!" works even better.

"Terramai" is the literal translation of *Landnever*. Something James M. Barrie never used, which is just bad English, not something that was ever there to begin with, but my parents would like it: I think this error is more faithful to what a child would say; it restores a joyous sense of escape, and as I rewrite the story in my head to include this word, I'm imitating my parents' daily acts of linguistic defiance. Translation is also a story of poetic imprecision. In this game, my parents always win.

As much as my mother liked watching Sanremo, she despised the purely musical aspect to it. There were never subtitles for instrumental sections. No attempt, no effort whatsoever to describe what was going on in the rhythm, if it was slow or rapid or dreamy. The only symbols appearing on the screen were: ♪ ♫ ♫.

Those notes meant nothing, were like writing a a aa bbb ///——cc and assuming these represented something in the absence of a shared code. Those notes were just neutral icons tossed in as distraction, to keep my mother in front of the screen without really having her there.

It was only later that I started thinking about those notes and those lost sounds.

In movies and TV series, the subtitles indicating a sound property, sound captions, are minimalist but effective [scary creaking] [heavy storm] [old man crying]: these formulas characterize noises through physical objects and adjectives that a deaf person has learned to decode over time.

The sound a text communicated would get a physical reaction out of my mother: a reference to a ghost would be enough to scare her; a hint of a storm would make her uneasy. The subtitles were innocuous in appearance: in Western culture, they're barely considered at all, are just white marks on black backgrounds, in anonymous typeface. They rarely include different fonts, any movement or color, any means for words to slip into some other aesthetic dimension; usually they show up at the bottom, unless they're covering up some necessary visual detail. But what if a character on the screen is writing a letter or typing something out? Wouldn't it make sense to synchronize the emerging words with the rhythm of the typing? The subtitles could also scroll down the side of the screen, one letter appearing at a time, or disappearing into the background, a pulsing flow of letters.

I wish poets always worked on subtitles; I wish public television would hire a whole army of surrealist or language poets who could make the blood run from a 𝖘𝖈𝖆𝖗𝖞 𝖜𝖔𝖗𝖉 in a horror movie, or make words disappear when they're said by gh ts or cross out ~~angry words~~ or sweep them away or make a statement pulse like a heartbeat if someone on the screen deserves it.

But most of all, I wish they'd quit with the formatting that makes absolutely no sense, like:

[woman whispers]

DON'T TELL HER I TOLD YOU

Who whispers in all caps? And how do I explain that to my mother?

We've never been to a concert together. I've taken her to see musicals, plays, ballets, movies, but we've never gone to see a live band. There'd be no point to this—except for a Beyoncé concert, maybe, with all the fantastic dancing and special effects—concert venues in Italy rarely have interpreters in a Deaf Zone: there is no Deaf Zone.

The last time I went to a music festival in America, I purposefully visited that area below the stage, prepared to feel like an outsider, since I don't speak sign language, a choice my parents made for me.

All the CODAs (children of deaf adults) I've met know how to speak it. One of my mother's friends has a daughter who's ten and knows how to sign in both Italian and Serbian; she's always teasing me when I'm not able to follow their conversations and I draw shapes in the air that are entirely made up. I haven't taken any classes to learn sign language, but I do try my hardest to come up with gestures that the adults around me might understand. Usually with disappointing results, and my mother will beg me to stop signing while we're out; she says I'm like some crazy dancer who's just been booted out of a company.

Dancing, that's what everyone did in the Deaf Zone: the interpreter's performance was impressive, but really, every language is a performance. Though unlike my attempts, her performance was coordinated, graceful, and most of all, meaningful: French philosophers are always obsessed with finding subjects that can "embody the text": they should pay more attention to sign-language interpreters at music festivals. American Sign Language interpreters translate incredible amounts of hip-hop, country, and folk music; every day there are more and more videos on YouTube that reveal what goes into this art form. The interpreters—usually women—especially love working on hip-hop pieces because they're so challenging, with every line break-danced.

Jay-Z is easy to translate for someone who knows American or Italian sign language, but what about wordless pieces? How likely is it for a deaf Italian or American to be exposed to Finnish ambient music or to African psychedelic rock? Who visually interprets these pieces, and for whom?

In 1979, John Varley published a science-fiction novella, *The Persistence of Vision*, about a drifter who tells the story of a world in collapse. One day, he comes across a commune made up of people who are deaf, blind, and mute and have developed their own linguistic code, *bodytalk*, with words spelled directly onto the skin. The protagonist becomes friends with an "able" girl, one of the few who can see and hear in this community. But her ability is relative: the girl doesn't know how to articulate the signs her parents mark on her body in order to communicate, and she doesn't know how to translate the words of the outside world for them. The members of the commune also speak through "touch," a physical linguistic act of sorts, where people establish contact through the body but with no sexual gender, no country of origin, no ethnicity, because they all communicate with each other while never being seen or heard, only through the sum of years and experiences that have rendered a particular body, where the skin is the story and every scar is a verb.

John Varley's deaf and blind people are empathetic, deeply fair, and devoid of prejudice; they deserve to govern because of their disability; in a utopian world, we'd all be imperfect and work together toward the common good.

It's nice to think about, that a sudden disability leads us

into a different relationship with power, will make us fairer, but my parents aren't anything like the deaf people in this novella, and I don't kid myself that they are.

I wish an interpreter of non-Western music could help my mother enter a transitional realm made up of bodytalk and synesthesia, where the hierarchy of the senses is constantly challenged and reshaped, so a piece of Finnish ambient music might still hold all the power of its own cultural landscape while dissolving into the familiar.

The surest way to translate sounds for the deaf is through technology. My mother's parents and brothers were visionary in this regard: the Walkmans and ordinary CD players they bought her may have been inadequate, but her family was on the right track. She needed add-ons to hear what they heard; she didn't necessarily need to see music to experience it: she could also touch it.

I have a piano at home, which my partner plays, and my mother will set her hands on top and say she can hear it, and I believe her. We may be listening to two different things, but I wonder if they converge somewhere, if at some point, what's visible of a sound might blend and dissolve into what's invisible.

Various high-tech companies are experimenting with special sensors that cause sound to travel through the skin, transforming the body into an ear stimulated by a sequence of vibrations. Technological transducers are becoming increasingly popular in the non-hearing community, but I'm bothered sometimes by their literal nature. Once again, my love of figurative language clashes with my parents' craving for materiality.

A fact is a fact, and a sound is a sound.

Subtitles and sound captions are interpretations. And they're intrinsically ableist: we're the ones who choose what noise or rhyme or applause is meaningful, based on what our hearing body perceives. We're the ones who decide what to include or not in this representation, we're the ones who create a disruption between silence and non-silence for the other who feels these things in a different way.

How do we represent this silence, our silence, if not by writing [silence]?

The Italian record label Alga Marghen released a record titled *Sounds of Silence—The Most Intriguing Silences in Recording History!*, a collection of incised silences on vinyl from Crass, John Lennon and Yoko Ono, Afrika Bambaataa, and other artists.

According to the liner notes, "These silences speak volumes. They are performative, political, critical, abstract, poetic, cynical, technical, absurd. . . . The LP presents the silences as they were originally recorded, preserving any imperfection that the hardware conferred upon the enterprise, without banning the possibility to [*sic*] satisfying the ear. . . . This album is meant to be played loud (or not), at any time, in any place: a true aural experience!"

In the last silence I experienced—the perfect silence of Doug Wheeler's semi-anechoic chamber in New York's Guggenheim Museum—I heard my own swallowing, the imperfect sounds of my imperfect body. Before going in, I couldn't truly understand the disorientation and vertigo my parents experienced, the same vertigo that made me seek shelter by the walls, like I was under attack. They tried to tell me, to explain, but I always turned that information into something else. Distance, usually.

Language is a technology that reveals the world: words are flames that we hold close to the inexpressible, so it might appear—as though reality were written in invisible ink— without words. Gestures are what make this translation possible. Maybe that's why I tried to learn how to use them, these words. Faced with silence, with the white, advancing shadow, I've raised my written pages and my parents, their tired vocal cords. At times we hurt each other quite badly, but we did so in an attempt to understand one another.

I can't build a semi-anechoic chamber and pretend the silence we share is the same, but like John Cage, I can tell my mother about the sound of my blood, and she can tell me about the sound of hers.

Snow in June

At age sixty, after a vacation in Greece (he's always gone to tumoral, hot countries in the summer and come home unrecognizably dark), my father had an aneurysm. A strange, bacterial aneurysm, the source unclear, and he collapsed and had to be hospitalized. They needed to open up his head, but he didn't understand how serious this procedure was and before they rolled him into the operating room, he asked for a cigarette or "at least a glass of red wine."

My brother called me from the hospital in Italy to tell me there was a good chance our father wouldn't survive the operation, and he wasn't sure how he felt about this.

How can we suffer for someone when all we really share is a biological intimacy?

My brother, by nature, is a fence mender, but even so,

neither one of us knew what to wish for. I took a flight from London that kept getting delayed, so I was forced to wander around the half-empty terminals until midnight, and I went for sushi in a restaurant with tinted lights and spent an insane amount of money. Before boarding, I locked myself in a bathroom stall and took a series of selfies that I looked at only after I fastened my seatbelt. I hadn't seen my father since he'd come for a visit and we wound up in a Chinese casino in Leicester Square, both of us too dressed up, and him buying me cocktails while we sat at the bar. He always managed to make me feel like a bookie's girlfriend.

At the hospital, the doctor explained to my brother and me that our father could wake up a much different person, and the worst outcome for him wouldn't be motor paralysis but damage to the speech center of the brain. Finding a speech therapist qualified to rehabilitate a deaf person struck by aphasia, typical in ictus cases, would be difficult, especially in Umbria.

When my father was awake again, his limbs retained their motor function; his body had come out intact. And he'd lost exactly what the doctor was worried about: his ability to speak. For days, he expressed himself through furious gestures and emitting sounds of deep rage. He tried to get out of bed and couldn't. He recognized my brother but not me. In an uninspired moment, I brought him a travel issue of *Focus* and tried to get him to write something down, but all he could make were hieroglyphics, which he then crossed out with a black line.

He had the looks, the features of an animal, and sometimes he scared me; I sensed a violence to him that hadn't been there for a long while. He couldn't find the words, but he didn't want to draw, either, and he'd stare at the inert dictionary. Sometimes he'd point to me and gesture to the doctors and my brother, asking who I was. Then one day, while I was sitting next to him, he spoke. He looked me in the eye and the first thing he said was: "Let's go to Paris."

From that moment on he slowly, painfully recovered a kind of speech, riddled with entertaining semantic errors.

During his convalescence, my brother and I would text each other on WhatsApp as we attempted to decipher our father's secret code. After taking many cracks at it, we figured out that "Fiorentina," his favorite cut of steak, meant "ATM." The word "work," which he had no reason to use since he hadn't done it for years, became "subway," though he never took one.

By now he's regained the meaning of nearly everything he says, and the only troubling remnants of that time are his suspicions that Jesus Christ and Hitler aren't actually dead. Right after the surgery, he'd wander around carrying articles or books on the topic, on the lack of witnesses able to prove the demise of these two historical figures. Perhaps he was suffering from some strange case of identifying with them both.

My mother nearly died ten years before him, of a heart attack brought on by smoking. I saw her jolt beneath the defibrillator and had to run out of her hospital room so I wouldn't throw up. When I asked the heart surgeon if she'd survive, he told me that he couldn't be sure. That it had snowed the day of his wedding, in June, and ever since, he couldn't say anything was certain when it came to his patients. Some had been released from the hospital and all was well, only to die in their car in the parking lot.

After their close calls with death, my parents haven't gone back to being whole—they're like time bombs, and I can sense they're about to go off from many kilometers away. For a short while I felt compelled to forgive them both: I kept seeing them under that defibrillator, that respirator; then time went by, and I forgot.

The Language of Dreams

My mother has a friend who's pregnant. The doctor tells her they need to do an amniocentesis, and she and her husband are scared about the risks involved. They're on a video call with my mother; she doesn't know much about it, but from her research online, it seems like the test would be a mistake—they shouldn't risk the fetus to determine if it has any disorders. My brother and I jump in on the call; we tell her friend she needs to have the test done right away, to make sure everything's all right. My mother, who always told us not to have deaf children, to choose if we could, ends the video call without saying goodbye.

"So everyone has to be born normal, like you two?" she blurts out.

When we suggested that her friend should have the

amniocentesis, we weren't thinking about the future parents or their new child: we were thinking about the daughter they already have, what it would be like growing up with two deaf parents and possibly a disabled brother or sister. I could just picture her at college, far from home. She was a great student, but with the shortage of economic and state aid for some families in Italy, I knew something had to give. When it came to my mother and her friends, my brother and I were among the few of the children who wound up going to college; nearly all of them worked after high school, to help out at home.

Some lives are foreseeable. Like heroes and heroines in novels are foreseeable. Usually, the disabled are protagonists in gothic or horror novels, or in the Gospels. These are the literary genres they've belonged to historically. In novels, a disabled character doesn't get to have a life like Franz Kafka or Emily Dickinson, doesn't get to work at a post office or in seclusion: a disabled character must be a genius, or have a voracious sexual appetite, or—not to fall back on the stereotype of one's goodness owing to one's limited state—a disabled character must be heinous, as cruel as a Shakespearian king. And the mute character, well, the mute character always plays the same part: the prophet.

There was an elegance to being mute, a visionary quality, a mysticism that I was suddenly jealous of as a child. At first, when the mothers of my school friends called me "the mute's daughter," I'd be furious and even pick a fight, but I soon realized my mother would be better off if she were mute— she'd get more respect, be considered almost a saint.

My wish that my mother was mute flared up the first time I saw Jane Campion's *The Piano*. We watched it together in prime time, and I started going through this imperfect identification with the main characters of the movie: we, too, were a mother and daughter; we, too, were immigrants in a hostile, unpopulated land. My mother didn't know how to play the piano, but she did know how to paint, and she hung out with the wrong men. But while Holly Hunter was gorgeous, regal, graceful, my mother was rude and disguised as a man. I did play tricks on her and take advantage of her condition, like the daughter of the main character in the movie, only there were no tropical forests, no steaming pools for me to hide in. The beauty of that movie lashed at me, left visible marks.

Perhaps, in a different sort of society, my parents would have different powers. Although there's only one power they truly want: to feel sorry for others. Their disability was a reason, an instrument of compassion, but my parents were almost never agents of empathy. Who could they feel compassion for? To my parents, real happiness is getting to exert even a meager amount of pity. Sometimes I've put them in a position to do so, performed some acrobatic maneuver that upends our relationship.

When I was four, my father destroyed any possibility I had of becoming a strong swimmer or good at riding a bike. We were at the seaside, and he took me out to deeper water and had me do a dead man's float; I trusted him and then at some point he just left, and my fear of swimming, inherited from my mother, was overwhelming—it was like being inside a water coffin. During that same period, he tried to teach me to ride a mountain bike without putting on training wheels first like all the other fathers did, who'd then unscrew them on the paths. I scraped my knees and decided not to try again.

The morning of my thirtieth birthday, my best friend said she had a surprise for me, and she took me to Villa Borghese. I thought we were going for a carriage ride; she pointed to a pair of rented bikes.

She knew I was afraid I didn't know how to do anything in life—every conventional activity felt like an insurmountable challenge for me—and she thought learning how to ride a bike would make me feel more independent. I trusted this friend like I trusted nobody else, and when she pushed me along that tree-lined lane and said she wouldn't let go, I believed her. A few minutes later I was truly pedaling on my own, wobbling all over the place, happy, a lightness I'd never felt before. She'd grab on to me now and then, afraid I'd fall, and then I turned and told her she could let go—I could do it. She was about ten meters back, bent over, breathless, red and exhausted; I was sorry she was so worn out, but I was also grateful. I did a few little runs on the bike and turned around, screaming with delight, and she was laughing, the people nearby looking startled that I was making such a fuss.

A few weeks later, I went to visit my father at his brother's home in Umbria. Grandma Rufina sat beside me on a low wall in the sunshine. I was writing something in a small notebook on my lap when a plumber and his assistant arrived. They were two good-looking workmen, and my grandmother gave me a little nudge and whispered, "Put down the pen and paper." She told me to sit up straight and smoothed down my hair while she smiled at the men, hoping they wouldn't notice that I was such a bookworm.

My father pointed at the bikes in the rack that my uncle left for guests to use. "You're thirty years old, and you still can't ride a bike," he said to me, chuckling, and so I proudly got to me feet, sure of myself. I straddled a bike, ready to make him change his mind, I pedaled twice and fell over. I tried to regain my balance, tried two more times, but I was completely incapable, as if my bike ride in Villa Borghese had never happened. My father came over and got on the bike to show me how it was done, with all the self-assurance in the world. He circled twice with no hands, sneering at my inability. I went and sat back down on the wall and watched, thinking that he'd won, and that was fine, I could let him have this. I could do that at least.

It's a variation of the game I play with my mother every month. A few weeks after getting her monthly pension, like clockwork, she'll ask me for twenty or forty euros. I just give her the money now, no questions asked—I know she's bad with money—so I won't add to her frustration: my mother's life lasts only a few days, from pension-euphoria to depletion, then returning to hibernation.

Then I invent some emergency to get my money back: clients who haven't paid, a sudden medical cost, the phone bill. I'll ask her for fifty euros, which she gleefully sends, with the joy of helping someone who can't seem to handle her own finances. "Of course I'll send you some, honey, we always help each other out," and she'll be very lively on our video call, happy to do something for her absentminded, broke daughter, and I know this is the best time of the month for her, when I give her the opportunity to feel sorry for me, to think I'm the unlucky one. I never use the money she sends; I send it back when she asks, and that's how this has played out for years now.

The difficulty in having parents with disabilities is facing up to the fact that their condition will almost certainly go on forever, that they'll never leave this state their entire lives. Paul, my mother's brother, is losing his hearing and is dazed by this much more than she ever was—he's not used to getting around without this sense, but since this hasn't always been the case for him, it's also true that he'll never become deaf. The mother of a friend of mine has lost 70 percent of her vision, but she's never worn glasses in her life, and she's not blind. Neither am I, though I'm extremely nearsighted. When my old university professor said that for those who are nearsighted, "the natural state is blindness," that without the prosthesis of glasses or contacts they'd be disabled, I went home with a stomachache, aggravating the feeling I always have if I think about my weak vision: that in the Middle Ages, I wouldn't have survived.

The deaf people I know consider themselves, first and foremost, a linguistic community, and view themselves as having a differentiated status in relation to the rest of the population suffering from a sensory or motor deficit, but I'm less interested in their identifying with a language than I am with how much that language evolves over time. I wonder if our perception of disability changes, if the vocabulary we use to discuss disability changes, even over the course of a single lifetime, or a single person.

I know our lexicon for speaking of other bodily afflictions lends itself to change.

During a stay in Milan, I went with my friend Eloisa to the hospital where she works. We were headed down a bright hallway for the surgery ward, when we passed a glass door, and above it were the words *Cancer Center*, written in English. She told me that English was used to evoke a sense of efficiency, to reassure visitors and to increase the hospital's standing in the best-practices world ranking system. I found it inevitable to think about what being removed from a language might do for people when relating to their own illness, especially if they haven't mastered that language. For people unfamiliar with English, wouldn't this foreign phrase have a calming effect in terms of their own pathology, wouldn't it help them to think of it as less real? This same selective removal occurs with people I know who choose to go through psychotherapy in English rather than in their native language, Italian. Having your therapy in a language other than the one that's shaped you, in which you've had your emotional training, allows you to take advantage of your limited vocabulary in this new language, so you can cut certain topics short, and relinquish certain verbs, to relinquish going into the past. Many find comfort in this terseness—it makes them feel like they're getting to the point, while their command of Italian can push them into hiding behind baroquisms and periphrasis, narrating their experience into fiction. A kind of therapy that's great for writing novels but not so great if you're trying to keep from killing yourself.

I often ask Umberto, a psychiatrist friend of mine, about the relativity of malaise throughout history. I ask him about the past treatments for borderline personality, something that can be traced to some of the women in my family, including me for a while. He tells me that forty years ago, a person like me would have been in for a little "frying." That's his exact word, "frying," and I burst out laughing. I sometimes treat him like a priest and confess that in spite of understanding the ideas behind anti-psychiatry, for a long time I wished my father had been committed to a mental hospital, when he was overflowing everywhere.

And I've also wished to force my mother's life, to shove her into the labyrinth of a classifiable disease, a wish that was constant when I was younger. Years ago now, the psychiatrist I took her to see, to discuss her manic-persecutory disorder, asked me a pointed question: "Do you really want to sedate your mother and erase every jolt of her personality, rather than intervening in her psychosocial marginalization?" I kept quiet and stared at the wall while my mother told me she'd never forgive me for this visit to the nut doctor, but what I thought was: "Yes yes that's what I want yes."

It's easier to say my parents are deaf, more complicated to

say they're mentally ill. Easier to say that my mother doesn't hear anything than to say she hears voices. These "voices" (known in the pages of biomedicine as tinnitus) are a disorder of the ear and result in someone perceiving hissing and prolonged vibrations. A constant ringing that can even drive hearing people crazy, and for my mother—who's not sure how to recognize these sounds—they become the voices of the dead, who talk to her from morning to night, or else the ultrasounds of some piece of equipment running in the distance. Every doctor I've brought her to has told me her case falls under a very obscure branch of medicine, where deafness, physical disorder, and mental illness conjoin. Doctors aren't sure what to do in cases of non-hearing people who suffer from tinnitus; it takes patience to try and divert their attention from that sound, but my mother lives on her own almost the entire year, and that sound is all she has.

Usually those appointments ended with a doctor's concise comment, "It's amazing she didn't kill herself," which is not what I wanted to hear. They could tell me my mother suffers from synesthesia, but what is the synesthesia in disability? The contamination of the senses is a privilege for us "normal" people. The only way I can make myself feel calmer about this is to think of it as "a very obscure branch of medicine," like parents do when their children have a very serious genetic disorder; the fact that nothing is known about something can sometimes be consoling. It's not a matter of a personal failing, that I can't cure her. It's that no cure exists.

How You Are? You're Tired
Tanti Baci Tuo Dad

Separation affects every child. Mine comes from inflections and inaccessible figures of speech; every irony separates us, every metaphor puts some distance between us.

I reread the letters my mother sent me when I was in college or the essays she helped me write when I was little, and this is always a gloomy affair, with me trying to defend myself. Because as I go through these letters, I'm forced to admit how many words she's lost, every adjective that's disappearing, every verb she doesn't really remember how to conjugate. Like Michael Ende's *The Neverending Story*, and the princess who could disappear if children don't tell her tale and the magic surrounding her existence: if my mother stops talking constantly with someone, if she lives alone all day, she loses entire territories of meaning. This is what's happening to her, withdrawing into the land of her illness, inside the castle that I'll never be able to enter.

It takes physical effort, this affection, this tie that binds us. Talking with my mother for days in a row means the constant transition from her linguistic universe to mine; by the end of the evening, I sleep twelve hours straight, my brain rumbling with broken syntagmas. Speaking slowly is frustrating, repeating the same concept over and over makes me want to hide in my room and not come out until she's busy with something else. I tell her it's exhausting, and she tells me that's normal.

That I feel tired. Sitting across from each other in an airport café, she says, nonchalantly, "Sure you're worn out— you've been speaking Chinese for a week and didn't even know it." That's what we're reduced to: my mother, protecting me from the pain of not being able to understand her anymore, turns herself into a different continent.

I've held on to so many of her grammatic and language errors; I still call an iron a "stiro da ferro" instead of a "ferro da stiro," like I used to in school, my teachers marking me down in red ink, and my syntax is often contorted—my one remaining tribute to her.

My mother's letters are reduced now to WhatsApp messages in acronyms: *Ily—tomorrow, live, you'll tell me— luv—it's an abstract thing.*

When she wants to say something is beautiful, she says it's

an abstract thing. Which my brother and I always tease her about. "It's an abstract thing" covers everything: the ending of a movie, a painting, the birth of her grandchild, a dress in a shop window.

In Italian, the verb "sentire" includes the experience of feeling as well as a specific sense: hearing. But in English, "to hear" and "to feel" are two different acts. I don't know how it works in other languages. And I'm not sure what I could do to translate those times my mother is lying in bed, eyes closed, murmuring, "Non sento niente"—how little "I feel nothing"/"I hear nothing" means to me, this cleaving in two.

OK Ti Love You

I've always thought my parents were different from everyone else, and then came the internet.

Teaching my mother how to use the internet has brought on a lot of disorder. ISIS has come into her life, along with cake recipes, diets, and animal torture. Her Facebook page is a triumph of anti-enlightenment, so she's now a part of the majority force of our time: she's not the only one voting for shady characters. My feelings about this are complicated. I worry about the false information she shares, and I'm horrified by some of her xenophobic attitudes (which she immediately counters with her Marianism), my mother, who's been a migrant all her life. But I also feel relieved, because for once, my mother seems entirely integrated into the world.

The information society has only reinforced her arcane

perceptions; the internet has become the place of Nostrada-
mus, a future crumbling into technological obscurantism.
We can't be sure who's teaching her to use emojis, acronyms,
slang; we're not sure how she's learning them, and this alarms
us. My boyfriend tries to discuss politics with her, to discour-
age her from believing everything she reads online. I see how
much effort he puts into synthesizing the information he finds
to persuade her to be more rational, then I see how she nods,
watching him, smiling kindly, so he'll understand that he's
right—she didn't know, she won't make that mistake again—
and as soon as he turns around, she's back at the computer
posting news on earthquakes willed by some South American
shaman.

For a while, she'd go on Facebook just to post a solitary,
laconic letter, a Q, an X, an M, a Z. No explanation, no
comment, her status would just be a letter of the alphabet.
With each passing day, those letters started to creep me out,
and I worried she was the victim of some chain letter about
to conjure up a black Mass. I asked her what they meant,
and she said the letters didn't mean anything. "What're you
supposed to say on Facebook then?" she snapped at me, and
there was nothing I could tell her: I don't like Facebook,
either.

Just as trap music has been reduced to chloroformed,
repetitive bass, to amniotic, Dadaist sequences of nothing,
maybe what's written on social media will atomize into my
mother's single letters.

I should just admit she's right—she's a visionary, in her

way: she was ahead of the entire world with her fake views, and the entire world has become my mother. Literalism, taking everything as is, confusing the signifier for the signified, this has always been her way, and I'm starting to feel increasingly drawn to the prospect of that dimension where she lives, where all you do is read the headlines. I can feel an amniotic pleasure in living in the same sac as my mother, where every bad thing just means a bad, feckless thing. I've spent my life resisting Southern Italy, resisting magic, just to watch them come pouring out of me, like water from my mouth, in every political situation I don't know how to withstand. I've chosen a different career, yet there are days when my mother's conspiracies, her whole life revolving around diets and platform games, are endlessly consoling.

My mother is always the same, but I've been the daughter of different women. At first she was handicapped. Then she became disabled. For a moment she was differently abled, but we're all differently abled. At one point she was just a crazy lady. Today she's someone on the internet.

Interrupted Girls

I don't recall the first time I saw a girl, interrupted. Maybe I was playing outside my grandparents' home in Brooklyn, on a street closed off to traffic, and she was sitting on the steps a few buildings down, with bandaged wrists. Or maybe it was the woman wandering with her shopping cart, the one who lost her son in Vietnam and collected returnables on Sundays. Perhaps it was my high-school teacher who loved the theater. Or maybe it was owing to Winona Ryder in *Heathers*, or to my mother, who let me watch *Fatal Attraction* with her when I was only six and while Glenn Close was boiling up the red-eyed rabbits, told me, "Some women go crazy. And who can blame them."

My reaction to seeing them was always the same: "Make sure you don't turn out like that." But what I didn't know yet was that for a number of years, I'd do everything I could to achieve the opposite.

My third year in high school, a creeping, black creature came to call, clinging to my body, climbing up the bed to my neck, but just once, then I chased it off, and my malaise took other forms. I don't trust books in first person that don't talk about these close encounters with monsters and the hereafter. But my training in the dark didn't make me particularly sensitive to the fears of others, and there are entire hells that I've missed.

For quite some time, I didn't realize my cousin Malinda, who I spent my summer vacations with in New Jersey, this girl with red hair and goldfinch bones, was actually addicted to narcotics. I'd get in the car with her and never worry about her drugged-out driving—I was jealous of her independence, her white Mustang that she bought at sixteen with her beauty-salon earnings. She'd grab some strands of my hair and hold them up to the light, and pass judgment: "Too many split ends, too dull—you need to drink more water," but instead of doing my hair, she'd disappear with her friends.

On the eve of her twenty-sixth birthday, she was out of suppliers. They were all in prison or had gone home for vacation, and her addiction—courtesy of a bad back and the opioid, OxyContin, that her doctors prescribed—had taken a desperate turn. To the point that she knew she had only two options: she'd have to sleep with someone to get her pills, or else check into a clinic. The tendency of American doctors to prescribe OxyContin is a sort of conscription into heroin—at least 30 percent of American high schoolers have tried a de-rivative of some kind. The media calls this *the opioid crisis*, like it's an exotic epidemic that hasn't yet reached our shores, distant-sounding, innocuous. Malinda has told me it'll be over in maybe ten years, that oxycodone isn't just casually sold like it once was, but there are still bodies to atone for, a generation that's been sacrificed and must now work through its own dependency.

Her predictions remind me of something photographer Nan Goldin said: that oxycodone is to the current generation what HIV was to her friends in the eighties.

One of Goldin's last photography projects is about her own addiction to Oxy, which lasted three years. The drug was prescribed for her tendinitis while she was living in Ber-lin, and after the legal scripts stopped, she had a New York dealer FedEx it to her. Like my cousin, there came a point when she switched to heroin because the quality-price ratio was better. "All work, all friendships, all news took place on my bed": what kept her going wasn't so much the desire to get high as the fear of *not* getting high, the terror that her body would rebel and she wouldn't be able to hold it together. I compared these recent photos with the ones in *The Ballad of Sexual Dependency*, her photo book about her friends in the seventies and eighties, in red rooms with filthy sinks, on beds, lying back like Marat murdered in his tub, only here the subjects are dancers and con artists, their lives at night. In Goldin's self-portraits from that time, of her posing with a black eye, you could always tell something was going on: the trauma was obvious—without that injury, the photo wouldn't even exist. The same goes for the snapshots on drug addiction: there were so many signs of ruin, the bodies on display already tragic. These new photos, instead, show Oxy for what it is. Nothing seems to be going on: the ritualized bureaucratic life of addiction involves a barely perceived desaturation of the person, at least at first. If I hadn't read the caption, "Self-Portrait 1st Time on Oxy," I would never have noticed that Goldin seems a bit more out of focus than normal, that she vaguely resembles Tom Waits. The point isn't that these portraits are any less beautiful: the point is, they're less overt, and so they faithfully portray this particular drug use; the colors here are of the hospital and the lighting is bureaucratic, because this drug is bureaucratic, state-run.

Once, out of pills, Malinda called her best friend to take her to rehab. She managed for a few days, then asked her father to come get her out of there. The snow on the way slowed him down. If my uncle had reached his destination, she would have kept on with that same life, but a veteran addict came into her room while she was packing her bags and told her, "If you walk out that door, you won't be back," and so she stayed.

The first thing she did after joining Narcotics Anonymous was to come visit me in Rome. I went to pick her up one night at Fiumicino, and when she stepped out those glass doors, I felt nauseated seeing her so skeletal, with her wasted features and nonexistent wrists. "Now I look like a dope fiend," she said, laughing as she slipped into the back of the car. She explained her theory on the drive: it's when you stop getting high that you get all the scabs and pimples, and your hands start peeling and your nose keeps dripping. When the body forgets its own addiction, that's when you have to face up to this horror, like when the person you love stops answering your letters or phone calls. The light goes out of your eyes, your hair goes brittle, you can barely spit out your words, and your voice just sounds like a refrain. "When you're on drugs, you're so bright and alive," she said, scratching at her nails.

She wanted to travel, had lost too much time, and so we traveled. Rome, Paris. We entertained ourselves by finding Narcotics Anonymous meetings where she could speak English. We'd check their websites for scheduled meetings, to see if family could attend. Some of her NA girlfriends had come across an app that told you where famous people went for their meetings; they spent an hour driving to flush out the singer of Depeche Mode in some church meeting room in Manhattan, sure he must have their same problem. And in a way it was true: they did have the same problem.

In college, one of my dearest friends took me home with him to see where he grew up. He lived on an enormous tree nursery in the Marche region, in a villa with the plaster falling off the walls and white geese all over the place. I knew his father became an addict as a boy, and most of his veins had closed; only a couple were still open and he treated them with care. "He's saving them for retirement," my friend joked. I was shy walking into that somber living room with its half-closed curtains; I felt like a king was about to receive me. His father got up from the couch and came over, lanky, his hair snow-white and thick, a style that looked like it hadn't changed since the eighties. After shaking my hand, he started talking about David Bowie's Berlin Trilogy, and I walked around the living room, lulled by his low voice.

When my friend and I discussed our parents, we discovered a number of similarities. Even if drug addiction isn't classified as a lack of some ability, is treated more like a form of generalized amnesia, both our fathers had this very similar trait, of telling us, "I'm not here."

His father died a few summers back, which I learned over social media; my friend posted a picture of himself holding his father in his arms and all these feelings churned inside me. He'd wound up paralyzed in bed and had decided to tackle all the books he never finished. I sent my friend a short email and we agreed it was a nice way to leave for the other side, disappearing behind a series of imaginary doors.

For some, ending a drug addiction was like ending a love affair, but the saddest definition I ever heard came from a woman at a meeting in South London. She said her life had been one long procession of car wrecks. One day she was caught in the twisted metal of a car, and she forced her way out and was trying to clear her head there among the others who were injured, whispering in the dark. She wanted to go somewhere crowded, and she got into another car and had another head-on collision, and that's how it went all the way down the road. At the end of the meeting she said: "You can control the effects but you can never break free of the symptoms," disavowing everything I knew about recovery—that you could become a new person. There was something perverse about the mantra they repeated at meetings, a perversion I didn't understand: "Once an addict, always an addict." So they wouldn't forget who they were, how they were made: if drug-addiction was a form of amnesia, sobriety was an excess of memory. Like injecting themselves with something that kept them submerged in formaldehyde, a taxidermy of sorts where they were always at the stage of the tracked animal, but in a forest without predators.

Theirs became the bodies of saints and martyrs, displayed on the square, to witness their suffering, to be an example, with no hope of resurrection.

Sometimes Malinda took me to meetings in small northeastern coastal towns in America, because these meetings were the most lively. "These aren't just burnout kids who dropped out of college and took drugs for kicks: there's some real tragedy here—burglaries, broken families, bankruptcy. Plus they're more ironic and spiritual." One of the burnouts sat down next to me at a meeting; he'd just been released from a mental hospital and was insistently tapping his feet. He asked me how I wound up there, and when I explained I was just a relative, he gave me a wicked smile: "You'll never know."

My cousin was right, there was something spiritual as people took the floor and told their stories about improving and relapsing.

One man finished telling his story and someone shouted *amen* over and over. He'd broken his habit after breaking his leg—they'd kept him in the hospital a long time. It was actually the reason he'd become an addict in the first place: the doctors had prescribed opiates but wouldn't renew his prescription once he was addicted. Heroin in America emanates from the health care system: one hit to get out, another hit to get back in, and in between a long, feverish forgetfulness. Rehabilitation forced him to get better, and when he checked out of the hospital he even started jogging. He ate avocados and wheat germ, avoided fried food. He wanted to do everything he could to stay healthy. But he did it for one reason only: "All I could think of while I was working out was that I had to be strong again so I could get high. My body had to be indestructible, so I could give myself over to drugs again."

I've never forgotten how he put it, that he wanted to surrender to opiates; I haven't forgotten this, this lucid giving oneself over to drugs.

And being there, I understood something more about love, and also about myself, that people, not substances, have a power over me. At the end of the meeting, the moderator asked: "Is there someone here who feels a *burning desire*?" and I sucked in my breath at those two words. Malinda and the widowers around me started laughing and were ready to get to their feet; I wanted to raise my hand to say that's what I felt, that this *burning desire* was my disease, though it's left my veins intact.

Yearning is an idea that I hate to translate into Italian, because the unraveling of *yarn* is completely lost, all that longing coming undone like a skein, like spilling your guts for love. In *yearning*, there's also something of *burning*, but my mother was wrong when she said that drugs were similar to an orgasm, because orgasms end, but when we fall into addiction, we never know if it will end, and we hope it never will; once we're unwound, there's no coiling us back the way we were.

Malinda and I were both fond of someone, this kid much younger than us, who signed an incredible record deal the same day the bank seized his parents' house, forcing them to move into a trailer. Chris managed to survive high school, even if he didn't have a nice car and lived in the dumpiest part of town. In some ways, he made it even without taking drugs or covering himself in rose-laden tattoos.

"I haven't changed," he said. "I'm the same person I was back when I was twelve." He was showing us his wardrobe, five white T-shirts and five black T-shirts, that he kept in the trunk of his car, before we went and watched his father shooting at cardboard flying saucers in the backyard.

After we took a walk through the rubble left by Hurricane Sandy, I sat down on a spring rocking horse on a childless playground and Chris got up on the roof of his car and pointed at the neighborhood, in a rare display of emotion, my cousin silently looking on. "It's no wonder the hurricane destroyed it all," he preached up at the sky ready to pour down water on top of us. "Christ, what a place." True, it would have been easier to let it all go, swept away in the water. Before we left, as he spoke of all the deaths he'd witnessed just during his time in school, he told us: "These days, an unmarked body is something to be ashamed of."

In thirteen years of therapy, I've always been in that ambiguous zone between possibly dying and never fully living, like so many others, maybe all others. Of the ten signs of borderline personality disorder, there was a time when I exhibited eight. The border, in me, was already drawn, and I've always been asked to cross it: every time I walked out my mother's door, I entered a different world, and I had to learn its tricks and codes, its beauty and systems, only to trade them in for something confusing and approximate every time I stepped back inside. At some point, I lost my way. A part of my life was invisible, unspoken, and for a long while, I couldn't say what it was.

Adult life involves a series of transitions that often include the scrutiny of your body and your psychological background. If I started the process of adopting a child, for instance, how many social workers would check out my arms or wrists? At a job interview, what chance does an ex-convict have who sliced himself up in his cell? Those in charge, the experts, see people who hurt themselves; I see people who are still standing.

All of you, try to make careless, distracted choices about your body when you're teenagers or still intact. The wrong bra, that'll make your breasts sag; the quick-fix diet to leave you with a web of stretch marks like craquelure over an oil painting; holes, tattoos, expansions—try to make choices that will seem wrong, to acquire a body that's not a conquest but the sum of its incisions, a braille of mistakes. And try to think of it this way, always.

I used to believe that to talk about human beings meant you had to talk about buildings collapsing, girls thinking they were skyscrapers destined to implode in an internal terrorist attack. But when I think of certain lives, all that comes to mind are old-fashioned geopolitics, classic versions of Risk! left to molder, with nations ravaged by pain, but still with impregnable strong-holds, condemned to resist, convinced the siege will pass, until they alone are left standing, their surrounding body becoming a state, with them its single dictator.

It's hard to talk about these bodies left standing; you're always reminded of a country at war rather than at peace, of Vietnam, which is never California.

I once wrote to a friend: "I hope whatever apocalypse you're killed by is glorious," but an apocalypse requires a co-herence that humans don't possess: for most of us, disaster is inevitably incremental, a daily accumulation, and before ever seeing its effects, we'll die, happy perhaps.

WORK & MONEY

What effect has poverty
on fiction?

—VIRGINIA WOOLF

A Worthless Novel

In 1990, *The Secret Diary of Laura Palmer* came out, written by Jennifer Lynch, the daughter of the director of *Twin Peaks*. I don't know how it wound up in my home; all I know is that in elementary school, after reading about Laura's adventures—hanging out with the wrong people, getting hypnotized, skinny-dipping at night—I started to keep a diary, a habit I pretty much held on to until I was twenty.

This diary wasn't the chronicle of my adventures and daily woes; it was an accurate record of falsification: it talked about cigarettes I'd never smoked, and boys I fell for but only referred to by their first initial followed by an emphatic period, and I was so dogged about composing this parallel life of mine that my mother was convinced, from sneaking into my room and reading my passionate descriptions of smoking in the bathroom, that I was hooked on nicotine by the time I was ten.

So, as I did in elementary school, drawing a fake house I didn't live in and writing essays about my family like a compulsive liar, when I visit my mother over Christmas holidays, I'll reopen these diaries and flip through the fantasy life of a girl who never existed, filled with clues to the person I was.

My mother has been working on a sort of autobiography ever since she was born, poured into journals, spilled into letters, piled high with a trash heap of phone messages: it's her complete works, and it consumes her more than anything else. I only have free access to one of these items, the diary she left with her friends before moving to America, except then she changed her mind and met my father. It's a farewell diary of letters, dedicated to a girl about to change her life, but then she doesn't. I know these friends' letters by heart, and there's one in particular that always hurts, from a boy in love, who writes: "You wanted to come to Rome, you came, and now you're leaving. You wanted a job, you found one, and now you're quitting. You were dying to talk with your friends, and when you got together with them, you almost never talked. Whatever it is you're looking for in America, you won't find it. I don't know if I'll still be here waiting for you, but if you want, try and look for me."

I know it by heart because it's a letter someone could also write to me: I didn't just get my coloring from my mother; I also got my obsessions from her, my inconstancy.

My mother didn't move to America that year; she saved my father on a bridge, and they had a son.

One day, walking along the embankment of the Tiber, pushing a stroller, my father beside her, she ran into that boy again; he was out with his girlfriend. There on the sidewalk, he turned white, she froze, but they didn't say hello. That letter tucked inside her diary is the closest she ever came to receiving a declaration of love.

Autobiography—and my mother's is no exception—is the bastard genre of literature, at least according to the old cliché of the literary elite: to these readers, it lowers the threshold, is fodder for anyone, refugees, women, people with disabilities, Holocaust survivors, survivors of all kinds.

Years ago, on Facebook, we spoke of ourselves in third person and this felt right, like narrative; we became characters and no one was bothered by this; then we went back to *I*, to publishing in first person, but the idea of making ourselves important through autobiography seems dirty, and we're back to harboring suspicions about the genre, though every day we reinforce it with our contributions, rendering it a collective autobiography.

A life can be thrown off course through different diaries. Mine was, through my mother's diary, and Laura Palmer's, and then through the diary of Bronislaw Malinowski, the father of modern anthropology.

In my first college lecture, the professor who'd be teaching our introductory course entered the classroom with his wild white hair and a bunch of papers under his arm and started talking about the connection between anthropology and literature. He told the story of Bronislaw Malinowski and how he founded the method of participant observation with his monograph *Argonauts of the Western Pacific*, which was destined to become a reference point for his colleagues and for generations of anthropologists to come.

But in 1960 something happened: eighteen years after Malinowski's death, his wife decided to publish his private diaries, those written during his travels in the Trobriand Islands, apparently against the wishes of his children and his colleagues, who feared it would be catastrophic to the discipline if these writings came out. In these diaries, Malinowski talked about the "holy urge to fuck them all" (meaning the Trobriand Island women); he described "the natives" with contempt, complained about his travels, and revealed his anguish over masturbation.

To me, it was like the professor was giving us a mandate to get drunk in class, shrug off our exams, and write bad poetry.

Those pages started and ended with Malinowski's thoughts on the writer and painter Stanisław Witkiewicz, or Stas, his best friend from childhood, whose friendship he lost. At one point he and Stas traveled together, then the First World War broke out and Witkiewicz returned to Poland; their paths separated. Stas wanted to devote himself to his country, while Malinowski wanted to pursue his ambitions in isolation.

In a very touching passage about his friend, he wrote: "I sometimes try to forget Stas. To escape him. I won't delve into the depths of his condition simply out of a selfish instinct for survival . . . I try to convince him with topics that I myself perceive as trivial and meager. Nothing is true, only death. But I can't, I'm under no obligation to go any further, to follow a friend to the last gates of Hades, unless it's to convince him to turn back."

I'd come to anthropology with Conrad in my heart, only to discover that his writing was haunted by shadows and to come across other Poles like him: Bronislaw Malinowski and Stanisław Witkiewicz and their story like so many other friendships. During one lecture, my professor said that true suicide isn't dying, it's burning your own diaries. At some point he used a particular word, *finction*, to define something that wasn't false but built up, a plankton also growing on my autobiographical notebooks in the attic. That word, I've never found it again, not in his writings or anyone else's.

But this relationship between Bronio and Stas, which ended badly, this I'd see demonstrated for myself: during my years in college, ambition would often reveal itself as abandonment, betrayed affections.

Back then I did a lot of obsessing over what friends I should have. On the morning I registered for classes, I noticed a diaphanous girl with red hair; I'd never seen anything like her. In the south, people's features were different; even the rich and refined looked somehow rugged. A few weeks later, when

I saw her sitting by herself on the first day of class, I sat down beside her and did everything I could to draw her interest. She dropped the major, went for political science instead, but I wound up choosing her. In a contemporary-history class that challenged my worn-out sense of American patriotism, there was a small girl sitting in front of me who had the coloring of Snow White. She was wearing workmen's overalls, and she swung around and told me, "You know it was Kennedy who initiated Vietnam," when she heard me talking about his commitment to civil rights.

All those students seemed better defined, more assertive and grown up than me; there was this one gorgeous girl, an anarchist, who got a urinary-tract infection in a Swiss prison after a protest to save the wolves or maybe over some state construction project.

I constantly asked myself how to go about being young while knowing that you *were* young, how for some people, time was never looking back with regret or nostalgia, and it wasn't ever feeling intensely anxious about the future, either; it was just *right now.*

I'd gone to college to find a father, a guide to shape and demean me. I faced every oral exam yearning for a bad grade, a "You could do better." I was looking for punishment, but no one took responsibility for improving me, except my friends, those studying alongside me: it was their seriousness and arrogance, far more than dozens of monographs, that launched me into the world. All the knowledge I sought was vertical, descending from an authority figure or someone holy—I was, after all, brought up Catholic—I'd find this knowledge in those like me, students also hungry for discovery, who over time became a family.

The story of Bronislaw Malinowski and Stanisław Witkiewicz terrified me and my classmates; it seeded all our fears: that to be brilliant, you had to fail and be rejected, and that an academic career and success, if we ever got that far, would only demonstrate our mediocrity. And in the meantime we took our different paths, the echo of that first lecture working its way into us, haunting us like a ghost.

There was another aspect to Malinowski that troubled me: his habit of reading really crappy novels. "As always, my narcotic is a worthless novel." In his diaries he talked about reading easy novels like they were heroin, a habit to avoid, a constant erosion of the principle of self-improvement. We read bad novels in our spare time, too, but it was a long while before any of us would admit this. We would never own up to reading memoirs.

Before finally killing himself in 1939, Witkiewicz threatened to commit suicide a number of times, a weight Malinowski found unbearable. I easily recognized it, this weight: I'd watched a few people attempt that leap, and then I kept seeing them around.

During my time at college, numerous stories emerged of intimacies and intellectual love affairs, like that of Margaret Mead and Ruth Benedict, who invented visual anthropology because she couldn't take notes and so her notes were what she filmed or photographed. Ruth Benedict was hard of hearing, and her contribution to the discipline of anthropology, her genius, was born out of her physical limitation. No one ever mentioned this in class.

Suburban Bourgeoisie

I discovered I belonged to a social class in college. When I lived in Basilicata, I was only vaguely aware of being part of the underclass.

The Caritas group tied to the church summoned us once a month to pick up food donations from the EEC, vacuum-sealed packs of rice with black welfare labels, generic cans of legumes. Astronaut food, which would last for all eternity. But since there was so much aid that arrived and there were so few people asking for it, the church volunteers would just hand out food right and left, and I'd wind up seeing these same poor-people cookies in my classmates' cupboards, so in the end this didn't necessarily indicate you were poor. Living in a small town in Southern Italy didn't help me to figure out my social class because along with everything else, our poverty was strange. In Italy, children of limited means didn't go around in Nikes, like my brother; they didn't have seventy original Barbies; and they didn't board a plane once a year for New York. At the same time, those children I went to school with always had food and didn't resort to eating cereal with water, or feel hunger pangs standing in front of a nearly empty refrigerator, with too many days left until the disability-pension payment arrived. That's because theirs was still a peasants' poverty of Southern Italy, tied to modest agriculture and buffered by family. Ours was also buffered by family, by our relatives in the US who bought us trips and shoes, but we couldn't always count on this, and most of all, we didn't have the stereotypical requisites for being dirt poor in Italy, what was necessary to be the "right kind" of poor: humility and a lack of pretenses.

Because pretenses we had, and more than anything, we were worried over our place in the modern world. In the darkest economic moment of my mother's life, when her children were in college and learning the trappings of spending, my mother took out an expensive subscription to Sky TV. It was her way of not giving in.

On a tip from my brother, I once watched an episode of *Shameless*, a show about a messed-up Chicago family. In one scene, the main character props a chair against the washing machine to keep the broken door shut, and I was watching something my family had done for years: we lived in an apartment where things used to be new and when they stopped being new, there was no way to replace them.

As for me, my poverty consisted of not being able to lead a life like most of the people I knew, especially my classmates. Poorer than them, but surely not as poor as those I didn't know. Our entire existence was defined by debt: to our grandparents, our friends, and then to our significant others. Here's where we fell on the indigence scale: poor enough to always have to call someone, but not so poor that there was no one to call. What exactly would you call that social class? My brother would say "parasites," a joke, yes, but plenty of people probably thought so.

After I got over my discovery of the "truly rich" at Sapienza—those who prided themselves on attending a public university—I thought that once I entered the workforce, class distinctions would grow opaque, instead of propagating in sneaky and even violent ways.

I started attending publishing events, shy, afraid to be caught out—an infiltrator. I had the right clothes, a phone like everyone else, but I'd worked to get them, and money simply wasn't in my family's DNA. The thing that worried me the most was someone learning about my Dickensian childhood and then clapping me on the back and saying: "We really admire what you've done with yourself." I was doomed to discover that the enlightened bourgeoisie was dying to know where I came from, and why. What had bored me to tears, they found a source of entertainment.

From 2009 to 2011, I wound up organizing cultural-studies and philosophy seminars in Istanbul for my employer. In practical terms, I booked flights and did the PR. At night,

I'd dine with the seminar guests, who were true intellectuals aside from being truly rich, and one time I found myself discussing my doubts about my social class with a Yale professor, an expert on human rights and moral philosophy. After I'd explained myself, this professor looked at me warmly and said my *little match girl syndrome* was misplaced, because where I was now, the point where I'd arrived, class didn't count. "Don't you see where you are? You're in the middle class, like all of us."

Our tablemates laughed warmly, nudging me, and in the end, I yielded.

But when would I truly feel I belonged in the middle class—when would that moment come?

I wait for that moment every time I make a motel reservation and get excited over the pool, and pack my swimsuit. As soon as I arrive, I drop my bags in my room, but when I go down to the pool, I find no one else is there, though the pool is filled and appears clean. So I'll wait until later at night, if it's open twenty-four hours, and I'll go down and swim and sit by the poolside. Even if my boyfriend's with me (and for him it's just an American swimming pool, a desolate, romantic thing), I can't help but feel alone: for me that pool is still a luxury. Just a girl's fantasy, and that no one else wants to go confirms this, because the truth is, this pool isn't actually that great, and everyone else just stays in their room. And so all my longing to dive in, to stretch out on my towel and shut my eyes under the neon signs bathing me in a red and purple glow, feels suddenly naive, like my eternal yearning.

I wait for that moment when I'm walking the aisles of the supermarket and I notice the packing tape, that tan, translucent, plastic tape and its unmistakable sound when unrolled; my mother used it to seal up the cracks in the windowpanes and to attach the broken handle to the refrigerator. We kept a stockpile in a trunk, and the whole apartment wound up that tan color. Every time I move or pack some boxes, I think about my mother repairing our furniture with tape at night, then falling asleep on the couch with the TV on and the subtitles out of sync.

Sitting next to that enlightened professor, I didn't know what I'd become, but I knew for certain what I didn't want to become: a woman who valued rising up from the bottom, or to start living the yachting life and forget where I came from; instead, I wanted to be a person who explored all the possibilities in between. And thanks to the welfare state, I've succeeded. Over six years, I received roughly thirty-five to forty thousand euros from the Italian government in the form of lodging, scholarships, and university services. The government set me free, permitting me to travel and become a young woman who could express herself like her peers. But she kept eating like she was poor.

Great Expectations

You eat like you're poor," my first and favorite employer told me.

He was the editor of a philosophy and cultural journal that was popular in the nineties, then shrank to a lofty Norberto Bobbio readership, on its way to extinction. He had a nice, well-lit office with terra-cotta tile floors and walls sagging with books, in the historic center of Rome. Our first meeting was a bit rocky. It was on the day of orals for my Political Journalism class—I'd skipped the lectures; we had the option of showing up at the exam with an English text and bypassing the normal syllabus, so that's what I did, I showed up with that book.

He was impressed by my dual citizenship, was an Americanophile, like many other editors of Italian journals. "Everyone's asking me for a job. Except you. Why not you?" He handed me his business card, and I left that examination room in a daze, not realizing this banter would divert our relationship along bumpy paths.

For my interview, I dressed the way I thought a war correspondent might or some classy yacht-club woman; I was hired at once. I spent those first days at work concealing my life and pretending to be more well-read than I was. We'd often go for lunch together; I'd order avocado and salmon—I thought this made me look refined—and ignored the venison and French cheeses. This is what drove him to say: "You always order the worst thing on the menu." He once also said: "You never had time to become an anorexic, right?" And my response—"I was always too busy reading"—made him laugh, and he kept on eating. He'd ask this sort of thing to see how quickly I could come up with a witty reply; he liked how I reacted to him, and through this, he learned to need me.

I went to college hoping to find a guide who'd transform me, and then I met him, and every day he summoned me into his office and explained the Italian Left to me, why it was disappearing, and he devoted an entire issue to women's rights. But sometimes he told me stories about when he was young, about his philosopher friend who was handsome and awful and had a prestigious professorship at the university and was always screwing girls and destroyed himself with booze; he recalled those summers they were young bucks—vittelloni—on the Romagna beaches.

He knew he had insights but lacked talent, and this was

true. He knew times were changing—he was very good at find-ing opportunities, but he wasn't a writer, and that I aspired to be one filled his thoughts. At first because he believed I'd be deeply disappointed, then because I'd abandon him.

One evening an old man showed up in the editorial office, someone who'd once published a decent novel, then everyone forgot he even existed. He'd come to propose a new book, which had been turned down by a number of Italian publish-ers. My employer gave him a half-hour audience and was kind as he said goodbye. He joined me in the other room; no one else was around and I liked to stay there on my own until dusk. We chatted awhile as it grew dark. "You see what hap-pens when you don't make it as a writer? Be careful—not everyone can handle failure. You need to protect your heart."

He was, when I worked for him, a man of around sixty, exceptionally handsome, with excellent taste in clothes, and for a while we'd travel around Northern Italy promoting his magazine in various circles; every time I packed my suitcase I'd feel so grateful that he had me travel, that he was genu-inely interested in my opinions about the world. His num-ber showed up more than anyone else's on my phone. For three years, he was all I talked about: all that counted were his disappointments, his bad moods, his developing depres-sion at being marginalized by the newspapers, the foolish mis-sion of bringing culture to the most unexpected, forgotten places.

My boyfriend and my friends couldn't take it anymore;

my brother told me this was going to end badly, that everywhere I went, I tried to make a family.

I didn't tell my employer about me and my parents right away because I was afraid it would be off-putting—he thought he'd hired a half-American girl with an apartment in Brooklyn and hadn't guessed about my Lucanian upbringing—but also because I knew that sooner or later, he'd use it against me.

To celebrate my college graduation, he and his wife (a Central European princess who was our patron and involved in the art world) took me and others from the office to a restaurant where the politicians went. It cost a fortune, and so did the suitcase they bought me as a graduation gift, and it felt strange to see them so proud and so there for me, almost startled by their desire to support me. I'd caught them in a weakness, so ready to indulge in an affection that I perhaps didn't deserve. It was a frightening discovery, creating family ties where none existed; when I celebrated my graduation with my mother, I had to pay, and I didn't get any gifts.

They taught me how to behave in polite society, and said I was a natural. He in particular noticed how I was able to manipulate the people around me. I'd try to find out what they liked and then I'd keep talking until they were stuck like flies on flypaper. Something he taught me, like a narcotic. He kept telling me that I'd leave and that I'd betray him, but he did it first.

We were in Sicily for a presentation. I arrived at the home of a baroness who was dabbling in publishing, and I met them in her living room. She jumped up from the couch and came over to me with her arms outstretched, though I'd never seen her before in my life. "He's told us everything, all about your past," she said, grasping my hands and pulling them to her chest.

Once again, it felt like I was in a Dickens novel. "Who taught you to speak?" the baroness asked, as if I'd grown up in the woods before being adopted, and then I understood what I'd become: not the wild creature I'd dreamed of, a young, ambitious woman equal to anyone, but someone's pet.

By the time I walked into my employer's office to quit, months had passed with me waking up feeling sick to my stomach and falling asleep with a fever, every part of me longing to sever that tie. I sat there, eyes down, crying, and let the office secretary tell him; she was a friend, and she'd understood that I wanted to leave. He shook his head, started scribbling with his pens, then spoke: "All right. No one's keeping you. No point in crying." I got up to go, was at the door, while he kept his eyes fixed on his monitor, and said, half to himself: "If you go, who's going to take care of your mother?"

Then he added that a girl like me didn't get to have her freedom. And I knew I'd done the right thing, even if I was losing a well-paid job and would return to a life of debt, to making a life for myself that was just as unfree.

I sometimes talk about all this with my girlfriends, who are horrified by the hold this experienced, older man had on me. They'll start talking about the patriarchy, the conflict of interests, classism. The truth is I miss him sometimes, and if I could return to that sense of feeling protected, if only for a short time, then I would. No one else has taken on the responsibility of teaching me a profession.

Right after I was dismissed from another magazine for a difference of opinion with the editor, he emailed me to say he'd read my public response to that incident and was proud of me but also felt somewhat concerned that I'd learned the ropes a bit too well, and was forcing my hand somewhat to raise my standing. He knew me well—was he right, even if that wasn't my intention when I wrote my piece?

That email was enough to implant a seed of doubt; it made me want to disappear. I never emailed him back, and his message still pulses like a ghost in my in-box and leaves me feeling churlish.

I wanted to be pure; he said I was out to find the highest bidder.

The last time I saw him was at his new editorial office, far from the historic center. He showed me his office, downsized in ambition—it looked like a land-registry office. He complimented my light hair, the first time I'd dyed it this way. "Did you just go to the beauty salon?" he asked, and that comment on my appearance made me feel evasive, and I looked down, strangely shy, and then I understood the problem: he was old.

Those times his wife would say, "We have to stop him—he'll have a heart attack," I'd just laugh; he was one of the most vibrant men I knew. I'd seen him plunge into the water when it was forty degrees out and I'd stayed with his other friends and colleagues, watching him from the shoreline, seduced and frightened by that vitality.

I still feel an unusual, spiteful affection for this man that I wouldn't feel for a father. That power I no longer had: to make a man feel old and pensive.

For years, after him, all I did was plunge into my work, searching for proof that I was capable.

Free Time

Discovering the bourgeoisie was shocking for me, nerve-wracking, and afterward, everything felt like a betrayal. Especially my body: I'd improved, ate better, so why had my employer said I ate like I was poor?

In his article for *Nautilus* magazine, "Why Poverty Is Like a Disease," Christian H. Cooper, in high finance and earning more than seven hundred thousand dollars a year but born into extreme poverty in Rockwood, Tennessee, tells us he only broke free through teachers and scholarships and explains why the myth of American meritocracy is actually a fraud demystified by science.

Poverty isn't just a social condition; it's a disease that affects us on a biological level. A disease passed down from generation to generation, through genes and unforeseen forms, that conditions the body in ways that not even future wealth can remedy. Arranging everyone on the starting line in the same condition isn't always enough, because there's a difference hidden inside those participating in the race, a difference that's often ignored. In truth, it's this metaphor of the race that's the problem, this cliché that's difficult to give up: growing up poor doesn't necessarily mean wanting to get somewhere, at least where everyone thinks you want to go. It can also mean staying put in one place, if it's someplace comfortable, desirable, that guarantees you everything you need. It can mean being hungry, but not hungry for success, the way most people think. The very idea of putting *hungry* and *success* in the same sentence is a bit farcical, in this day and age. Waiting there at the starting line, a girl might just decide to head off into the woods. Her life might also be fantastically squandered; equality means setting her up to become an astronaut, if she wants, but also giving her the chance to be idle when she's not sure what she wants to do yet and writes articles for cultural magazines in the meantime, even without an apartment left to her by her grandparents. Equality means workers' children not just becoming doctors and lawyers but also underemployed writers and painters holding out to see if they have talent.

Often the poor who break free from their social condition have an auto-sabotage mentality that shows up as nostalgia.

My mother was proud but also bitter about my improved economic situation: when I worked at my office job, she always sighed and said, "Lucky you anyway," and I'd feel sad at how resigned she was as she fondly remembered her days working at Agip Petroli; when I quit my job, she ignored how bad I felt, telling me what a disappointment I was, an insult to women's lib. "What're you going to do—get a sugar daddy?"

I reacted by developing a disastrous relationship with money: as soon as I got any I did everything in my power not to see it, manage it, save it. I didn't want to start feeling nostalgic because I wasn't like her anymore, ruined and just as mournful. But I couldn't help myself.

Poverty is a blot in the cells, the smudging of one's DNA. Nothing realigns after an adolescence spent in need. You don't learn to eat differently, like someone who's not hungry. Every time I have to leave something on my plate because others are, or because I'm full, I feel my disgust take over, a violence toward myself, and I have to count to ten, or else I can't do it.

My eating betrays me. So has the disappearance of physical money.

The early part of my life revolved around a basic absence of cash. When something had to be bought, this involved a trade, a series of promises, verbal rituals, and negotiations that made money vanish as soon as it arrived, almost turning it into an imaginary substance. So when I started working, money didn't become something necessary, to be handled with care: for me, money felt slightly ridiculous and unreal, and I only got used to it over time. Then I moved to London and my money practices no longer held, because once again, physical money had disappeared: gradually, these past few years, withdrawing and paying with cash have stopped. I've gone from being afraid of not having cash at the supermarket to feeling embarrassed about only having cash: it's almost like my life from before, only now there's value in the invisibility of money, and I feel backdated when it comes to gain.

When I was little, my mother sent me out to buy magazines and other items at the newsstand; I put everything on our tab thinking that was normal, until my classmate, the son of the owner—the boy in elementary school who played Joseph to my Madonna—whispered to me: "My father says you can't anymore." We both were shy, we liked each other, and we never talked about this tab at school.

The topic of poverty doesn't hold the same weight for my brother, which demonstrates that belonging to the lower class doesn't mean being part of one gelatinous, indistinct mass with all its subjects laying claim to the same rights or memories. He distinguishes between objective poverty and the mishandling of one's money—the basic nature of our childhood and adolescence. But what is poverty if not the impossibility of making mistakes with money and calling your disfunction "eccentricity"?

There's a narrative of poverty that's tied to meek sacrifice, to dignity, to not asking for much. A version I maintained for years, bothered by my mother's spending habits, the things she bought but couldn't afford. A lot of ethnography work has been done on the impoverished segments of a population, less on the debt system and living above one's means, what sociologist Matthew Desmond defines as "eating lobster on food stamps."

And on the subject of the bureaucracy poor people have to go through, similar to drug addicts, all their trouble finding the necessary resources to buy things they've got no right to buy, this subject's been studied even less—it's just too brutally oppressive. That's because we don't just expect the poor to be revolutionaries (like they have the time for this, instead of spending all their nervous energy on figuring out how to obtain something, anything, by any means necessary); we also expect them to have good manners, to be on their best behavior.

I have a close friend who works in a cooperative that handles the repricing of secondhand goods, with most things going for one to four euros, to students and people with large families and migrants—but also to people who resell these items at Sunday markets. Not too long ago, she told me she feels like a failure when these people steal things off the shelves. Low prices, for the cooperative, are a way to create a network of kindness, to increase awareness about reuse, and to keep the supply chain intact. We had a long conversation about this, and I could understand why my friend was disappointed, but at the same time I wondered about the pedagogical expectation we sometimes place on thieves, how tempting it is to doubt their need, to misconstrue things, because we're bothered by their stealing.

My mother has always been a rude poor person who's lived beyond her means. A poor person with no debts is morally superior to a poor person with debts: I learned this from the Bible; I learned this from TV. Now, when faced with these teachings, all I feel is deeply suspicious.

I work, and I know I've never seen my parents really do the same.

I wasn't worried because they were unemployed and lazy, and this increased social prejudices against them; I worried because their inactivity made them sad.

I wouldn't be so concerned about how my mother manages her money, or I'd be less concerned, if it didn't make her feel depressed at times; if she had even a little of the poor, cheater's euphoria her relatives felt when they immigrated to America. Every time my parents have done something, sold a painting or some small piece of carpentry, the satisfaction they derive from this is immediately set aside, sacrificed to something far more important: the feeling of being tragic, defeated, rejected by the world.

There's something they both do that drives me crazy: they collect random items for art projects that they'll never complete. My mother brings home branches, stones, shells, and dried flowers; my father fills his garage with boards, tools, wire, and other junk. They each have a potential cache of beauty that they'll never use and that meanwhile gathers dust. My parents have no work, only free time, and they don't know how to use it.

LOVE

Every seven years, our cells renew:
we are now who we weren't.
Even living—we forget—
our time in charge is short.

—ANTONELLA ANEDDA

The Echo of a Mythology

S ometimes I think, if I had done such and such or I hadn't done such and such, that I never would have met Bobby, but that's not the point, is it? I mean, I would have met Bobby, always. Some Bobby or another. I was looking for him. I don't know if you understand what I mean, but Bobby made me feel necessary, safe." These are Helen Reeves' words in *The Panic in Needle Park*, a 1971 movie, with the screenplay by Joan Didion and her husband, John Gregory Dunne, inspired by a photographic essay in *Life* magazine about New York heroin addicts.

My boyfriend gave me the DVD as a gift when we took a long bus trip down to Basilicata to visit our parents; he made me unwrap it before we even left. We watched the movie over Christmas, like coconspirators, lying in the bed of my teenage nights.

When I heard Helen say these lines about her boyfriend, Bobby, something inside me collapsed, surrendered completely: like my father crossing the threshold from the movies to the street and not truly realizing it—his behavior farcical, hallucinatory—I, too, couldn't distinguish that character's confessed devotion in the film from my own feelings at the moment, in my room, half-draped over the body of another.

I couldn't be further removed from Helen, selling herself so Bobby could get high, or from Joan Didion and her cold fever that put those words in Helen's mouth, but I recognized both these women. And love, for me, was always a matter of recognition. That night, I fell asleep wishing Helen Reeves' words could be my destiny. The opposite of an exorcism ritual: I didn't want to use these words to break free from affection—I wanted to repeat them until I wore them out, an echo of repetitions and abuse, until they were forever true, the only thing that could be said about me, my character, my life vision: all those years I'd been inert, thinking I'd disappear, I was really only waiting for someone. I was searching for him.

The boy lying in my bed looked like Bobby in the movie. The same hollow eyes, same facial features of those character actors in the Italian American movies I'd cut my teeth on, with a slyness bordering on sociopathy. A body, a voice, that took me back to my childhood, but also the kind of body I'd worshipped as a teenager, the same physique as those English musicians, sickened by life, never really knowing how to play an instrument, so frail, so mortal, driven by jolts of sociability, out-of-sync electric bursts, a shyness pushing to the limits of inadequate confession, euphoric laughter and its true misalignment, its true splitting off from the world, something I alone understood.

A matter of recognition; that's all it ever was. And always would be. Like Helen said, I would meet Bobby, always. I was waiting for him.

· · ·

My friend Nikolai was sitting in a garden thick with vines; he was hunched over, on an orange plastic straw-bottom chair, like the kind you find in small-town bars with their old SIP pay phones.

Nikolai wanted to shoot pictures in a neighborhood full of fascist-era buildings, and I'd gone with him. Before we got to the bar, he photographed some graffiti on a wall: "Godot has arrived." I didn't find it particularly original, but I know he wound up using it as the title for a photo book. It was a nice collection, filled with men dressed like Tony Manero in his white polyester suit, walking teary-eyed through the night crowds.

He was a friend I wouldn't see again, or at least not very often. He'd just turned thirty and was telling me his heart was broken, tapping his cigarette into his still-full beer, telling me it was over with the woman he loved.

The first time I saw his girlfriend we were sitting, sipping tea in the lobby of a mosque, and all he did was point to her feet and ask me, didn't I think her sandals were beautiful. I did. Her shoes were gorgeous, and so was she, but I felt very sorry for them both. She was mostly silent, and was the second time I met her, too.

We were all sitting at the bar. My boyfriend had drunk
more than the rest of us, never changing expression, watching the bartender, who was taking half an hour to mix a
cocktail, as if this were a religious rite, at three in the morning, with customers nodding off in the corner. The bar
had dragon-blood red walls and dusty mirrors, and once we
stepped outside, about to head to our apartments and hos-
tels, it vanished.

Nikolai and I had spent the whole night talking passion-
ately and getting drunk, and when I hugged him and his
girlfriend on the sidewalk, it occurred to me that I wouldn't
be seeing them again, not together. I was a bit jealous of the
twilight sadness to them, but they weren't the kind of people
you really miss.

I spent the rest of that night throwing up in our bathroom,
my boyfriend holding my head and wiping away my sweat,
and then I dropped off to sleep, happy I had someone who
loved me and cared if I woke up in the morning.

Months later, in another bar, in another city, my friend
slumped over even more, eyes weasel-red and saying he loved
her so much that he'd lost his mind. His psychiatrists forced
him to quit, to stop harassing her; she'd threatened to report him.

Nikolai stared at me a long time, then said: "There's no
cure for love." Him and his goofy hysteria. "Oh, please," I
answered.

And what about me—had I ever loved someone so much
that I lost my mind?

The Love That Would Not End for Another Eighteen Years, If It Ever Did, Began

One day I'm seventeen, and I fall in love. I'm walking down the hallway at school, a nameless high school built on a giant parking lot, and I see a boy and I know he'll be important for me. My decision is unrelenting, fatal, will change my life and—in a world where relationships frequently reoccur, every love deserving a different kind of solitude—will make me differently abled in so many ways. But I couldn't know that back then; back then I was just a loud, lonely teenager, and I needed someone who was different from my parents but who also wouldn't make me feel ashamed of them, and it was immensely difficult to find someone to love.

What I didn't know yet, peeking at that scrawny, black-haired boy, was that like him, I'd confuse our being together with membership in a secret society, that we'd mistake sex for a kids' blood pact, like in any good summer read. And with that same sense of predestination: a love story is a self-fulfilling prophecy, and if the signs aren't there, then you have to invent them, so they become all-important.

Between high school and college, I fell in love like couples who married young after the Second World War, and over time, I started developing the nostalgia that the last of a species might feel when their own kind is extinct or about to become so, wondering if what I was doing with this other person, what he was doing with me, was just a less dramatic version of what had happened with my parents: they, too, at Trastevere station or the Sisto Bridge or whatever really went on, were just searching for someone to save them.

That boy and I both had charisma but no standing in school. I schemed my way into getting his number off a mutual friend, and we spent our afternoons that May talking on the phone. Then the day of my seventeenth birthday he showed up at my door holding out a bouquet, unable to look me in the eye. I don't think he liked me any more than I liked him. But there was some instinct that I'd never felt for anything else, a longing for conversion. We didn't really like each other, but we both liked to talk.

In September, when he'd already left for his first year at

college and the New York towers came down, I called him and over a long pause, I realized that love was also this, a lightning strike in the dark, a person to call during a disaster or coup.

My bones weren't even fully formed when I met this boy— you haven't stopped growing at seventeen. Technically, biology says you'll keep stretching out. So wasn't tying yourself down so early a way to stunt your growth, like binding a child's legs so they'll be stunted? From this point of view, even my mother was more normal than me: she had boys who pursued her, and one-night stands. Every time I heard my girlfriends bragging about their lovers and their strange night encounters, or later, when they made fun of marriage, I thought I was one of those women they were mocking, a suburban wife, certainly no heroine of my time.

There's a TV series that was still popular back then, *Beverly Hills, 90210*, and one of the main characters looked like Chris Chambers from *Stand by Me*, but a few years older. This was Dylan McKay, and when he showed up, one of the others would often say, "Hey, stranger." Dylan would come and go from school, would disappear on long trips, and every time he returned, someone welcomed him home with those words. Through bad Italian dubbing, "Hey, stranger" became "Ciao, straniero." And he, too, used that expression, "Ciao, straniera," with the girls he loved. First on Saturday evenings, then in reruns after school, thanks to Dylan McKay, I was convinced that love came with that principle of estrangement, of crystalized unspoken things between lovers.

"Ciao, straniera," Dylan McKay would say to Brenda Walsh, and that message, in all its lazy translation, I carried with me as a dowry; my own falling in love was made up of distance and I did all I could just to hear this phrase said to me, one day, through the lowered car window, an especially happy grin on my face, then racing up the stairs and plunging into bed and hiding in the pillow.

The truth is, the dubbing wasn't bad—it just wasn't how teenagers talk. But that's what books and TV shows were for, so when we heard such things, we felt all-powerful.

Lovers Have Faith,
but They Tremble

When Ethan Hawke and Julie Delpy found themselves on the set of *Before Sunrise*, the 1995 Richard Linklater film, they were concerned about all the dialogue the Texas director wanted them to memorize. It's not a film where much happens, really, aside from two young people meeting on a train and then all the hints leading up to their infatuation. He's American, she's French, they have one night and won't see each other again for another nine years, in a second movie called *Before Sunset*. Linklater told the actors that he had never survived a plane crash or been a spy or traveled in a space capsule, yet his life was filled with drama. And the most dramatic thing that ever happened to him was becoming intimate with someone. One day he met a girl and they talked all night, fell in love, and never saw each other again. From this he came up with his trilogy on the connection between human beings. All the conversation in the movie about politics, sex, dreams, and religion only serves to reveal "the space between two people."

Years later, Linklater discovered that the girl, Amy, who inspired his movie had died in a motorcycle accident in 1994, so she never had the chance to see him again. But what would have happened if they did find each other again, if they continued talking for all the years to come? How long before time came to obliterate them, for biology to take its revenge and make them two people who were once again strangers, far removed from that night?

After college and graduation came living together. Sometimes my boyfriend would wake up with long scratches he didn't get from me; we'd compare our dented sleep marks in the backlight of morning and laugh. For a while we were twins, neither of us knowing where those marks came from.

At night, before we went to sleep, I'd stare at the back of his neck, and he seemed like a gorgeous woman warrior, pale and covered in moles, with narrow hips and strange scratches he'd gotten all on his own. I'd jump up from the couch or run to the other room where he was working and say, "Isn't it great, being able to hold someone?," while clutching myself like an orphan. There were times, though, when we existed horizontally, stretched out on the floor or lying in the bathtub fully clothed, after our choreographed arguments in parking lots, when our longing and desire for the other were only proportional to our longing and desire to disappear.

The best discovery in adult life was the tender violence wrapped up in illness: My boyfriend has been sick three times since I've known him, and every time, my blood blazes and I feel revived, energized, as I take full charge of our domestic life; I'm endlessly pleased when he's helpless. As for me, I used to think getting sick was incredibly provincial, that if anything, I'd die from nervousness, but I spent many of my English years in bed claiming various ailments and asking him to leave the curtains closed.

The most meaningful moments of our relationship have happened on our long walks together, usually in port cities, in the red, malarial light of summer. I don't trust a person I can't take a long walk with, walking until our lungs are bursting and we feel stabbing pains in our calves; it reminds me of those walks to Lucanian towns with my mother.

There was a time, on a vacation in Los Angeles, when I felt we might live there forever. Our first drive into the city, we got lost among those islands in the highways—Los Angeles isn't an encampment, it's an archipelago with asphalt for water—and we popped in and out of the music stores of Little Armenia as we searched for the apartment we'd rented and held hands and never took our eyes off the street.

I'm not sure what was so special about those mornings spent walking around the hills, by the uninhabited houses, or our nights on the porch of our rental attempting to read in the polluted evening light, but for once we were silent, synchronized, animals. I don't think I've ever understood his feelings so well or anticipated his every move as I did on that trip, and when the time came to leave, I stood in the doorway of that apartment thinking we'd still be happy but never again like this, with this perfect intimacy composed of quiet laughter in the dark and eating Chinese food in bed, and sleepwalking through the valleys of this city overrun with plants we'd never laid eyes on before. An underrated, climbing city, devoid of any real center, and we were captivated by all its hostility.

Years later, after seeing *Doctor Zhivago* at the theater, we discovered that the snow in the ice palace in Varykino wasn't actually snow; it was soap flakes and pulverized aspirin and caused the characters to slip as much as ice. And the actors playing Lara and Zhivago weren't in Russia but Spain, and all the extras were afraid of singing "The Internationale" in the streets, in this country under Franco's regime. We discovered this in a winter full of a similar social disruption, while holding hands on the way out of the British Film Institute, and it was easy to raise the question: How many separations could Lara and Zhivago survive?

Sitting at a warm table in Peckham, to celebrate the new year, as though we had no relatives or religion, it was easy to think we would have been left unscathed by all the changes. We could see that movie ten times, and we'd never believe that palace in Varykino was full of crushed aspirin, and not snow.

Bobby or Another

A romantic bond, a love story, over time turns to dogma, like those of the Mormons, and religious fanatics, and families with seven children and crucifixes hanging in the hall, and fifties housewives ashamed of their own orgasms. A bond, any bond, after so many years goes against nature; ideology takes hold, and love's not a feeling but a discipline. It's something unmentionable, which we only want to read about if someone promises it will end, that turning the page, this love will only be a past yearning.

As a species, we're condemned to evolve, yet we believe that a relationship will stop us at some point, that there's a teleology in encountering someone, a certain someone. As if being a couple transports us to another dimension, where we can't become any more perfect or luminous than we already are, a protected space where we have no desire to betray the person we know, to sleep with someone we'll never feel close to. Forming a bond like this when you're young doesn't mean anticipating what's to come, but shaking it up, demystifying the idea of maturity as the defining stage of existence before others do it for you. An intimate rebellion against the laws by which we grow and become satisfied and unchanging, when we've always been departures upon departures: tears, sutures, and cuts.

What does a long-lasting relationship really mean? That your body freezes, you become a woman in a glass ball, hoping sooner or later to be turned upside down. I wanted to be cryogenically frozen, to see if I could stay in that love forever. When I failed, when he failed—*to fail someone*—I didn't just miss him; I missed the feeling of being immortal.

At a restaurant, we were sitting by a guy who kept talking to me, trying my patience, feigning a nonexistent intimacy. Or at a flea market, the owner detaining me, going on and on, and my partner walked out, waiting for me twenty minutes outside, and I was stunned and hurt that he wasn't jealous or even interested, and on both these occasions he just said: "I was waiting for you to realize you were being ridiculous." In another instance, when I'd convinced myself that I could live on art and desperation with a certain kind of man: "You and all those *artistes* telling each other stories about your tragic past—do you feel better then? All of you, so special, so alike," in an awful voice, and when this happened, I'd feel mortified, shy, ashamed of myself, but with his cruel—often true—

comments, I'd also experience a throbbing desire, that he knew me better than anyone and could predict my every mistake, knew every last one of my flaws, had absolute control over them, and I was won over again, on a Russian heath, with him not even bothering to pull out a dueling pistol, just dropping his glove and leaving the ballroom, and afterward, I'd never see him again.

He said that taking on me and my world was like Stavrogin's decision "to marry a crippled girl" in Dostoevsky's *Demons*; there's a long passage where he explains how he needs to be degraded to affirm something to himself.

In one of his favorite books, Philip Roth's *My Life as a Man*, there's also an element of subjugation, and I ask him to tell me about it. I turn off the light and say, "Tell me again," all the reasons why he can't leave.

Every day, I thought about being defined by my family, by my economic and geographic circumstances, and then I realized that it's someone else who's had the deepest, most decisive impact on me, someone I'm not joined to, not tied to by blood. I've never been to the moon or learned to swim or injured a friend in some duel, but I've met someone.

One day I started a conversation, and I never stopped. I might have come from anywhere on earth, been an alien condemned to never being understood, but then I started talking and someone heard me, and this has defined the form I've taken, has ultimately shaped my expression in photographs and how I pronounce my words. We might hold a secret etymological root, but who will decode it?

On nights we can't sleep, we say that loving each other is communicating in this private code that won't leave you even when you close your eyes, and how can you lose someone, if you don't forget that person's syntax even in your most exhausted dreams?

Desires become leveled out and uniform; insecurities remain varied forever.

His greatest, most mysterious fear is ending up in prison or else maimed. The loss of personal freedom is far more distressing to him than the loss of love. There's a cold, bluish kernel to his heart that drew me to him like a martyr.

"If I wind up dead on the floor, if I ever manage to kill myself, you'd be more afraid of calling the cops than losing me," I tell him, and we both know there's some truth to this. But we know his pain would come, maybe years from now, when he's traveling or when there's some especially beautiful dialogue between lovers on TV—then he'd remember the bond he formed, and unformed.

Ciao, Straniera

We live surrounded by salvation narratives, both when we're really happy and when we're not. Therapists, friends, relatives, everyone we've met over the years has gone on about what's healthy and what's not. Finally persuaded, we looked up *codependency* and *symbiosis* in the dictionary, how to cope with the need to find autonomy; we studied the entire taxonomy of love according to the DSM, and what we concluded from the DSM is that no one should ever love anyone, because there's no good way to do it.

It's like lichen that might be mistaken for a single organism but is actually two bound together: alga and fungus. Plant symbiosis is accepted as a miracle of nature; between humans, it's a fault or something to be ashamed of, a backward state of being. We've tried to separate and we're always thinking about how it will end—we've done this since day one. From the beginning, the idea of its ending has helped keep us together; we devote passionate science-fiction conversations to this, imagining the life of one without the other.

"We were better off when I was crazy and you were a fascist," I write him one morning during a particularly ugly period. "Nostalgia for our Years of Lead," he texts back, and for a few minutes these analogies I've used make me feel cheap, but then that feeling of desecration prevails, which has always been a part of how we communicate.

When I was a girl, I wrote him letters. I'd say I wanted to sink into a vat of photographic acids so I could imprint myself on his body; he'd say there must be a drop of my blood in his, like a bubble of ink dissolved in water. Back then, I'd lie down in the street because I couldn't bear walking anymore, and I really didn't know where to go, and he'd lie down beside me and wait. If I started to shiver, he'd lay his hand on my stomach and only then, with my back touching the asphalt and him touching me, did I feel that maybe I could start again, and have a life. We were never caught in someone's headlights, but I think even if we had been, we'd still continue to exist, pull ourselves up and keep on walking, sometimes close, sometimes distant, never unaware of the other's presence.

Sometimes when I'm wasting time, I'll go look up famous marriages on Wikipedia; I like finding a genealogy tree of suffering and betrayals; it becomes a mausoleum branching out inside me, opening into new rooms. I check the bios of women authors I admire, and I realize it's not that I want to write like they wrote—I don't give a damn about writing like them: I want to love like they did, fail like they did.

I grew up believing that if I entrusted myself to another, even if it was against my will, I'd be saved forever. A retrograde idea, dismissed in Western society, in psychotherapy—who depends on her partner these days? And if you do, you're ignorant, uneducated, weak—but a part of me still believes there's something important in retreating, in this lucid giving yourself over to another.

Sometimes my mother will spy on us from behind a door or window and she'll ask what the point is to holding hands; she insists we're too intimate even if we're just touching each other. She doesn't know what those gestures are—she never touched my father like that and she hasn't had a man since to try it out on. She's amazed watching us, and we feel embarrassed and tender at the same time. My mother always says that every woman has two great loves, though she's never even had one—at this point she speaks in soap opera-ese: "Now you have a secret, too—you're a woman. Don't you think he has a secret? Never forget you're a *person*."

He could tell her that he killed someone, that he participated in an orgy or robbed a bank, and she'd never bat an eye. She wouldn't know how to begin to tell us how to live, and we sometimes take advantage of her indulgence, lay scenarios on her that we don't even confess to ourselves, making her one more witness to our confusion. We try to draw strength from her experience because, even in the ruin of her body and in her solitude, she teaches us that a person can survive alone, and this is what we fear the most: discovering that alone and far apart, we'd actually survive just fine.

I spent last summer visiting friends who pumped milk for their children at four in the morning or while sitting by the pool; I saw their stretch marks, the blue veins on their legs; they say they don't recognize themselves anymore but in spite of everything, these friends have started living their lives while I've felt mine was headed into reverse.

At the point when everyone's taking on a marriage and a mortgage, I'm moving outside of time, I'm moving forward to go backward; every day feels like a negotiation to get through, to verify my existence without the body of another beside me.

I don't know how to carry myself out in the world, bodily.

I don't know how to say, "I'm alone." I don't know how to say this to the person with whom I've shared my body, deep in the night when I wake up and feel I'm a carcass they've only forgotten to silence and smother, and I ask myself if his body is also useless, a growth that's frightening to him, shameful.

After we've been apart, he tells me it feels like having sex with a stranger. Exhilarated at this discovery, we return to the subject of endings. We know how novels end but what about lives? Slowly the idea is raised that writing, like love, is something you can give up. You can tell a story, then quit, and walk away.

Sometimes we think only tragedy will cleanse us of what

we are, but this isn't true. When Grandpa Vincenzo died, the
first thing my mother did was take a shower. My brother
said: "Maybe now she'll learn to take better care of herself.
The shock of it might help." But that's not what happened;
my mother continued to decline, to wash only sporadically,
and to be depressed. I don't think there's any type of pain
that can put us back together again; I think it's the exact
opposite.

For my partner's birthday, we went to Danzig, where the
Second World War officially began. For three days, we visited
the city's museums, its galleries filled with placards on totali-
tarianism and twentieth-century ideology, and the Stutthof
concentration camp. As soon as we left the camp, despite the
gravity of this historical place, we started to fight. I was complaining about the stupidest stuff: the wallpaper in our house,
other ridiculous things; I set one foot in front of the other,
plodding forward in the grassy sludge of the canal, wondering how it was possible that even here, in the presence of the
atrocity of humankind, I still couldn't control myself and act
like a better person, instead of yelling like a crazy lady out
there in the Polish countryside, with strangers at the bus stop
watching us walk along, silent now in the cold, and me still at
it, hands stuffed in my pockets, never turning around.

In the taxi to the airport the next day, a Leonard Cohen
song came on, "Dance Me to the End of Love," and it felt like
a bad joke. I took his hand and told him it just couldn't be,
this had to be some kind of joke.

But that's the difference between us: I think the song's

about a passionate relationship between two people, and he reminds me that it's a song about the Holocaust. "Not everything is about love," he says, looking away. His face, like the rest of his body, no longer brings me back to my childhood or my adolescence: there's nothing gaunt or frail about him; he has a different bone structure now, is built like a man.

In that bar so many years ago now, the one with its plastic orange chairs, when my friend Nikolai said, "There's no cure for love," I'd told him to just let it go. He was referencing the title of another Leonard Cohen song, "Ain't No Cure for Love." I hadn't realized it then. Years later, in that taxi, I said the same thing to the person I loved, and he just looked out the window.

Next Time

I had a dream once that I was a monster. Like the scary creatures from when I was a child: I had red eyes, a sloping,
sensual body, but instead of attacking my victim, ripping him
to shreds and chewing on his neck, the only thing I did was
lie down on him, sprawl out over his back so there was no
space between us. And when my sad, inhuman skin turned
into this other person's skin and we began to breathe together
and no one could tell the difference between us, whose blood
ran in whose veins, that's when I woke up.

I was still a monster, but I was no longer alone: the greatest violence I've ever committed against another hasn't been
leaving a person or breaking his heart; it was turning him
into someone like me.

It's a terrible misunderstanding to think that vampires and

werewolves go out only in search of victims. If that were true, they'd torture people without absorbing any bit of them, just abandoning their carcasses on the ground, not caring whom they chose first, then abandoned. But anyone who's met a vampire or werewolf knows that's not what happens. People almost never die from these encounters. They stay alive, coexisting with what's missing: a drop of blood, a piece of flesh, a bit of brain, something of oneself that will shape the memory of another, the body of another. Becoming another in spite of yourself: I'm not sure if this act is sublime or degrading. All I know is the light emanating from this act, the depth of this light, is important to me. In the end, what's left isn't the magnitude of the event, the capacity for change or the damage it's caused, but the fact that it's irreversible, that there's no turning back. In my dream I wasn't a monster just because I forced someone to be like me; I was also a monster because I'd erased every memory of his life before me. If he tried to say any different, that he would have been someone before he met me, no one would believe him: my story was greater than his. If every one of you wakes up and you say you lost a piece of yourselves in the jaws of a diabolical creature, no one will stick around to listen. If you say that the remnants of this infection are with you every day of your life, maybe someone will show you some pity, but this person will never know what you're talking about. Try saying you're a monster instead, or that you always dreamt of being one: everyone will think you're right.

In 1989, a woman named Ada JoAnn Taylor confessed

to suffocating a lady in a small Nebraska town. This came after a number of sessions with psychiatrists who tried to get her to remember her past. They told her she needed to relax: if she'd only relax, she'd remember what she'd done; her memory might even return in her sleep. And so Ada JoAnn Taylor imagined, then confessed to being a murderer. In 2008, after nineteen years in prison, new DNA evidence brought about her release. She never committed this crime, even if she did describe it in great detail, even if she says she can still feel her hands on the pillow as she suffocated her victim. When they told her she was innocent, she almost went crazy. "If I can't even trust my own memories," she told a journalist after her release, "then what can I trust?" The world outside hadn't changed; it was the same world that thought she was right before and now thought she was wrong. But for the world outside, it's one or the other: you can't be both executioner and victim, both Dr. Frankenstein and his creature. It's useless for Ada JoAnn Taylor to tell people: "You can't say *I'm not* a murderer." But someone can say this to me. Someone can tell me I didn't destroy anyone, that even if I remember it that way, remember feeling the person I love splitting open beneath me, his body turning monstrous like mine, worse than mine, there's no truth to this, no divine order ready to decree who created whom. And to separate us, for this.

In our dreams, no one absolves us, no one condemns us. And how responsible are we for a life if we only wounded that person in our fantasies? My monster doesn't speak, and hasn't spoken for a long time. I keep asking him, though: if I was the one who created him, if I hurt him, if I'll ever be able to make things right. I'd like to tell him that he wasn't a coward, that he may have surrendered to my life, but I also surrendered to his.

WHAT'S YOUR SIGN

You are walking along a road peacefully.
You trip. You fall into blackness.
That's the past—or perhaps the future.

—JEAN RHYS

Gemini

I'm taking a walk with my mother in this city or maybe another.

I tell her it's her fault I stopped reading my horoscope. And I recall those lingering nights in her kitchen, in candlelight, with her arranging runes on the table. I'd scramble up her legs, and then she wrapped me in a towel, and I felt her warm breath as she checked her fate; it was my favorite way to fall asleep.

She reads some pages of my book and says I got it all wrong. Take the story of her great-grandmother—she left San Martino d'Agri and sailed for Argentina, then made her way up to America, working in nearly every country, spending a long time in Mexico, before she ever reached Ohio.

There, she met a family of Italian construction workers, and fell in love with the oldest son, married him, and when they both got rich and tired, they returned to Basilicata, sparking a migration that's continued ever since.

My grandma Rufina is going senile. Every day she covers herself in her jewelry, like a Byzantine queen; she says she has to enjoy all her jewels. When I come for a visit, she tells me about the Picassos she commissioned, but these are just paintings bought at the Porta Portese market.

My brother has a little girl. I watch her play with her grandparents; my father terrifies her, he's so loud; my mother, interacting with her, regresses into a perfect childhood, and makes me feel strangely jealous, and I wonder if she was ever this way with me. I watch my brother, the natural ease he has with his daughter, so spontaneously caring and capable. We come from mythologies of fathers and mothers, but no one ever says how much your whole body is tied to your brother—he's your first mirror.

There's one episode of an old sitcom, *Northern Exposure*, about a blood drive. The Native Americans of the show think you can recognize people by the color of their blood, and they look at all those piled-up plastic blood bags. If they put my brother's bag on top of mine, would I know it was his?

In New York, when I took the N line to Brooklyn, I'd catch sight of some old graffiti. On a downtown building, someone had scrawled: NEVERLAND. A billboard blocked it at some point, but for a while it endured, so I wouldn't forget and keep living stuck there in between, like some migrants who keep living in the country they left, sending a hologram of themselves for the future.

I've never actually been to Neverland (Neverland mon amour), but I've been past it.

When I was a girl growing up in my town, I checked a book out from the public library (the library that would eventually flood), a biography of Karl Marx. As a young man, Marx quoted a poet in the *Neue Rheinishche Zeitung*: "When everything collapses, courage remains." One day I was seventeen and thought I knew what it meant to fill the space between two people.

I discuss my parents with the niece of the woman who jumped off the Arc de Triomphe. I tell her they never wanted to accept being deaf, to give in to anything. "And why would they?" she asks. Not because they were deaf, but because they were young. We should never curb our desire to be something else.

* * *

On Oxford Street at Christmas with my mother, buying clothes she'd later regret, in a city where I can't measure the distance from home.

I asked her what her life would be like if she weren't deaf. "I'd be insignificant."

After years of describing herself as a victim, she also told me that everything that's happened in her life she chose for herself, and in this declaration, I heard, I felt her freedom.

I know I didn't disappear because someone found me before I could.

I've listened to my mother, and I haven't forgotten that I'm a *person*. I'm the daughter of a man who never jumped off a bridge: every time I feel myself hit the water, I rise. When everything collapses, love remains. But is it a true story?

AFTERWORD

Where do you come from, who do you belong to, how did you learn to speak.

I've been hearing this chant since I was a child, echoing through the caves and cracks of my life, and as I became a woman, similar questions rose to the surface, under the guise of greater sophistication: *Where are you going? When did you become yourself?* and *Does someone belong to you?* My answers varied, were made up and forgotten. I never felt this chant was positioning me or pushing me in one direction; nothing could really pierce me and make me spill out, my secret self buried deep below the conventions of identity and belonging.

But if a person is a map, where are the real crossroads, the real junctions, and is there any way to share these names with others, outlining an original and irreplaceable landscape called I?

Pretend to be writing yourself and researching yourself as if you were something that really happened, traceable in history and time. You'd study yourself as if you were a curious object, name the person who first discovered you, those who broke you, who reassembled you before you exhibited all this in a novel. For a while, you'd be led to believe that your main materials were other people: lovers and friends and teachers who settled to the bottom of you as sediment and turned your ideas into that specific color or shape, something extremely easy to present as proof of yourself. At one point, you'd be convinced that each indentation or scar or depression in your own body and being bore the name of a mother or a father—it had to be a mother or a father—but this is rarely all true.

The cracks you contain are not just family, history, or geography: fiction hurts, imagination hurts. Strangers you never met hurt, in celluloid and on paper. It's perfectly possible to break up with people, to never speak to a parent again, and to eventually forget them; I find it harder to break up with fictional characters I really cared for. I think this is what my drunk high school friend was trying to say when he admitted that the worst thing that happened to *him* was *my* father trying to kill himself on a balcony in front of the entire town. Unintentionally, this friend taught me a lot about fiction and the surprises that come with it, what we forget and what we hold on to: to this stranger, my father was fiction, and the impression my father made on him was not something I would ever experience for myself.

What follows is an incomplete list of published works that turned me into a character or a person, depending on how you see me. Genre, in the end, is just a game of possibilities and clues; it takes only a little misstep to slip out of a novel, to fall into an autobiography and resurface again as an essay, all in the short span of a sentence.

In my own primal dreams, *La straniera—Strangers I Know*—was meant to be read in nonlinear fashion. Ideally, every edition would present a different chapter sequence, as I believed this would affect the experience of the reader and make it clear that there is no obvious entrance into or exit from a life: in the end you would find many different books, susceptible to variations and second-guessing, as if you were reading a horoscope that's applicable to anyone and yet unique to every single person. While reading the horoscope that's so dear to my mother, you wouldn't always necessarily pick Love over Money over Health; you'd select what you wanted to read first, according to your own need or preoccupation at the moment. I wanted this preoccupation, this self-made experience of someone before the page, to be central to the story of my life. I wanted to expand the cells of the I and discover if they could be stretched to the point of shattering and not "mattering," literally, to the point of the self no longer consisting of matter, until the self dissolved into the memory of another, the life of another. This is what I've always asked of fiction. To be personal and anonymous, situated and universal, mine and everyone else's.

One question I never heard until this book first came out: *When did you realize your parents were deaf?* This happened only a short while ago, when I was in Spain on a book tour. A girl from the audience found a new entry point into the novel (Why hadn't I thought about that? Wasn't this my story, in the end?) and I was left speechless: In a quick rush, I traveled back into some room of my childhood and became

an infant, barely able to walk. I felt and imagined myself
staring at my parents while trying to find an answer. How
did I know they couldn't hear me? And then I realized I didn't
know—I probably never knew: I didn't perceive this on my
own. Their deafness was a story someone told me. Someone
pointed out a difference in my parents, and I started to branch
out, drawing the boundaries of where I stood, and where
they were. I wish I had a personal epiphany to confess, that I
could recall a sudden physical break of intimacy between me
and my mother; I wish I had a sensor revealing to me what
was different and what pulled us together or pushed us apart.
But that never happened: their deafness came as a story. And
so, to me, in some strange ways, identity is always a story
someone tells you about yourself. Personality or character or
selfhood—and not a perfectly crafted story—this is the most
beautiful simultaneous translation of all your desires and
lies.

You dive deep into your I, and you figure out that you're
not a map, no matter how wide you are, how marred; you're
never just a single artifact with a simple label, but a complex
and ever-growing crystal, with its light ever changing, and
ever capable of surviving time. These are my shards—all the
girls, boys, cities, sounds, and histories I could have been.

"After Great Pain, a Formal Feeling Comes," Emily Dickinson; *Oliver Twist*, Charles Dickens; *Music of Changes*,
John Cage; *Synthetic Desert*, Doug Wheeler; *I Am Sitting in
a Room*, Alvin Lucier; *A Scanner Darkly*, Philip K. Dick;
The Master, Paul Thomas Anderson; *Cool Memories II*,

Jean Baudrillard; *A Wizard of Earthsea*, Ursula K. Le Guin; *Automatic for the People*, R.E.M; *Stand by Me*, Rob Reiner; *The Body*, Stephen King; "Like a Rolling Stone," Michel Gondry; *A Letter to a Child Never Born*, Oriana Fallaci; "Lappin and Lapinova"; Virginia Woolf; *Grimms' Fairy Tales*, Brothers Grimm; *Last Exit to Brooklyn*, Hubert Selby Jr.; *Dracula*, Bram Stoker; Fernanda Pivano's translations of F. Scott Fitzgerald and Jack Kerouac; "The Legend of Sleepy Hollow," Washington Irving; *Léon*, Luc Besson; *The Paul Street Boys*, Ferenec Molnár; *Cuore*, Edmondo De Amicis; *Alien*, Ridley Scott; "Missing," Everything but the Girl; *The Confessions*, Augustine; *The Diaries of Judith Malina: 1947–1957*, Judith Malina; *Fahrenheit 451*, Ray Bradbury; *Lolita*, Vladimir Nabokov; *Land and Family in Pisticci*, John Davis; *Magic: A Theory from the South*, Ernesto de Martino; *A Clockwork Orange*, Stanley Kubrick; *Taxi Driver*, Martin Scorsese; *The Moral Basis of a Backward Society*, Edward C. Banfield; *Christ Stopped at Eboli*, Carlo Levi; *A Vindication of the Rights of Woman*, Mary Wollstonecraft; *Frankenstein*, Mary Shelley; *Max Payne*, Remedy Entertainment; *The Lord of the Rings*, J. R. R. Tolkien; *Please Kill Me: The Uncensored Oral History of Punk*, Gillian McCain and Legs McNeil; *Cudzoziemka*, Maria Kuncewiczowa; *The Stranger* or *The Outsider*, Albert Camus; *Bark*, Lorrie Moore; *Cultural Intimacy: Social Poetics in the Nation-State*, Michael Herzfeld; *The Exorcist*, William Friedkin; *Scarface*, Brian De Palma; *The Evil Dead*, Sam Raimi; *The Wonderful Wizard of Oz*, L. Frank Baum; *Peter Pan*, James M. Barrie; *The Persistence of Vision*,

John Varley; *A I A: Alien Observer*, Grouper; *Enforcing Normalcy: Disability, Deafness, and the Body*, Lennard J. Davis; *Sounds of Silence: The Most Intriguing Silences in Recording History!*, Alga Marghen; *The Neverending Story*, Michael Ende; *The Piano*, Jane Campion; *Heathers*, Michael Lehmann; *Fatal Attraction*, Adrian Lyne; *The Ballad of Sexual Dependency*, Nan Goldin; *A Room of One's Own*, Virginia Woolf; *The Secret Diary of Laura Palmer*, Jennifer Lynch; *Caro Bronio . . . Caro Stas: Malinowski fra Conrad e Rivers*, Alberto Sobrero; *Evicted*, Matthew Desmond; *Historiae*, Antonella Anedda; *The Panic in Needle Park*, Jerry Schatzberg; *It*, Stephen King; *Beverly Hills, 90210*, Darren Star; Before Trilogy, Richard Linklater; *Doctor Zhivago*, David Lean; *Demons*, Fyodor Dostoevsky; *My Life as a Man*, Philip Roth; "Dance Me to the End of Love" and "Ain't No Cure for Love," Leonard Cohen; *Good Morning, Midnight*, Jean Rhys; *Northern Exposure*, Joshua Brand and John Falsey; *Blood Bank*, Justin Vernon; *Stories We Tell*, Sarah Polley; *Marx: Eine Einführung*, Iring Fetscher.

ACKNOWLEDGMENTS

This book is dedicated to a girl and a boy who lived through their deafness with recklessness.

While I was trying to be brave or to be good, they were teaching me how to be free.

I hope I was able to mirror their recklessness at least in fiction and to finally become their "true" daughter in the realm of the imagination.

I would like to thank my agent and friend, Sandra Pareja, for reading me into my broken languages. We share a craving for landlessness and for many neverlands.

This book wouldn't have traveled the way it did if it were not for Rebecca Servadio and Camilla Dubini, early readers of *La straniera* and two women I strongly admire for their commitment to literature and beauty.

During the editing of the Italian version, Chiara Spaziani defended this book and its anomalies with all the bravery and confidence she has: I believe in open and shapeshifting texts that truly become themselves only through another voice and gaze. She was my first other voice and gaze.

There was a slow and strangely hot day in Austin, Texas, when I first spoke with Laura Perciasepe about what would become this book in English, and I immediately felt she would be a big part of this story and make it wider. Her intense scrutiny, passion for translation, and intimacy with the book have helped me sail back to America after many years of longing.

I am constantly grateful that she made it happen.

Thanks to Laura and everyone at Riverhead for trusting this voice.

To my translator, conspirator, and true pirate, Elizabeth Harris, who fought through these words with all the generosity and defiance I could wish for. It's been quite a ride, and she always had my back and saw things I hadn't originally perceived myself: translation is always a conversation with the invisible desires and leftovers of the original text. Thanks, Liz, for reading me so well and for being such a scavenger.

One day I met a boy. I told him I came from a family where sometimes no one was able to hear, and he slowly taught me how to listen. The writing in me would never have crawled outside without this intense faith in the art of listening, and all the endless conversations we had.

—*Claudia Durastanti*

TRANSLATOR'S ACKNOWLEDGMENTS

This novel kept me company during the difficult year of 2020, and I'm incredibly grateful to have been entrusted with its translation. Thank you so much to the people of Fitzcarraldo, Text, and Riverhead—to Jacques Testard and Alaina Gougoulis; and to Laura Perciasepe for her thoughtful, careful editing and her enthusiasm. My thanks as well to Kendall Storey and Sandra Pareja; to Louise Rozier for all her help; and to my patient, supportive partner, Scott Kallstrom. Finally, I wish to thank Claudia Durastanti for her beautiful novel and for all her encouragement and help with the rendering of this book into her "blueprint language."

—*Elizabeth Harris*